D0562112

# BLACKBEARD'S GHOST

These be ye words o Satin
O speek these words o
blak magic and bring
ye curse o Satin to
ye Goke Eden and
Tesy Magua
Writ in my own
true blood ye dog
burn at stake
Lady Aldetha
Stowecroft
January 6 1719

Aum Aum Aum
Manaman Verbum
Fohat Kali Yug

# BLACKBEARD'S GHOST

BEN STAHL

ILLUSTRATED BY BEN STAHL

SCHOLASTIC BOOK SERVICES

NEW YORK • TORONTO • LONDON • AUCKLAND • SYDNEY • TOKYO

Copyright © 1965 by Benjamin Albert Stahl. This Starline Edition is published by Scholastic Book Services, a division of Scholastic Magazines, Inc., by arrangement with Houghton Mifflin Company.

9th printing.................................................................February 1974

Printed in the U.S.A.

# CONTENTS

*For my wife, Ella*

# 1: PROLOGUE

JONAS PEPPER clamped his lopsided tricorn hat firmly down upon his gray head. He tightened the woolen homespun scarf around his neck and glumly observed the full moon skulking through shredded clouds.

Wheezing, he reached for the iron lantern at his feet. Its yellow flame guttered and smeared the frosty ground with a greasy light. Jonas held it level with his round face, examined the candle, and grumbled, "Ain't so good as them ye gits in Philadelphia Town, but it oughta last till the end o' the watch." He trudged down the middle of the crooked street between scattered houses that were lowering chunks of foggy black silence. The moonlight shingled the roofs with tarnished silver, and gray smoke wisped from distorted chimneys.

Jonas raised his bell and let it swing loosely, like a pendulum, at his side. It clanged rhythmically. His lonely cry was a monotonous long-drawn-out lament: "Two o'clock and all be well! Two o'clock and all be well! Two o'clock and all be well!"

Mournfully, the distant wolves replied. On the waterfront, the smells of rotting seaweed slime, of fish, tar, and hemp were strong, and over all was the pungent tang of the sea.

Jonas slogged along through muck, the debris left behind at low tide. His foot sank ankle-deep into a water-filled hole. He slipped, cursed, and almost fell.

Before him, cluttering the crest of a low ridge that paralleled the beach, was a row of shacks. Others, even more dilapidated, were perched on piles that extended a short distance into the harbor, silhouetted black against the brilliance of the moonlight on the water. Small boats of every description were either moored to the pilings or beached.

Jonas plodded past the ribs of a large sloop under construction. He plunged into the blackness between two log houses that reeked of fish, and his lantern bobbed, a flickering spot of orange. Emerging on the beach side, he paused and then slipped and skidded down the gentle slope to the water's edge. He looked across the harbor.

A large merchantman from Boston, the *Nancy Taplin,* rode at anchor. Beyond, on a silver strip of sand, a thousand sea gulls trilled and mewed. For no apparent reason, they flocked upward into the moonlight and circled, endlessly screaming, then drifted downward like falling feathers to the sand and the rocks.

Jonas gripped the handle of his bell and it clanged as he stumbled over the rubble. He squeezed his body between a broken river scow and a careened sloop. Oh, how he hated this part of his watch! He knew very well that if he was going to run into trouble, this would be the place. He hoped that evildoers would see and hear him first, and get safely away. Holding the lantern high, he rang the bell furiously, then paused, listened, and peered up and down the beach. He was just turning to go back up the slope when he saw it!

A phantom shrouded in black scurried from behind the scow, darted across a patch of moonlit sand to a low shed, and was instantly devoured by black shadows. A black cat came from nowhere, spat at him, and lazily bounded toward the shed.

Jonas sucked air through clenched teeth, dropped the bell and lantern, and reeled backward. He slammed into the scow. Barnacles cut his fingers unheeded as he clawed for support.

"Aldetha Stowecroft!" he croaked. "The Godolphin witch will be back!" Quaking at this omen of ill luck, he picked up the lantern lying on its side spreading a dying light. He was looking for the bell when, from across the harbor, sounded the grinding squeal of splintering timbers. Jonas forgot the witch; he forgot the bell.

At the entrance to the harbor, a hundred yards from where he stood, a large sloop with only the jib set was trying to force its way between two huge rocks that jutted near the end of the sandpit. The ship careened and ground to an earsplitting halt, the bowsprit high, as if pointing a finger of warning at the village of Godolphin.

From within the hull a pistol roared and Jonas heard a muffled howl of rage, then more pistol shots.

The gulls screamed and smoked upward, blurring masts and rigging like clouds of white confetti.

Jonas was petrified. He watched men spew from the hold, rush to the bow, and leap pell-mell into the sea while others scampered high into the rigging. He heard a wild bellow, followed by more pistol shots. A bullet whined. Alarmed, he scrambled behind the scow. More bodies plopped into the water as men threw themselves from the rigging in an attempt to escape the wrath of a bearded giant who stalked the deck, pistol in one hand, cutlass in the other.

The giant roared and screeched like a fog-horn. He climbed to the bowsprit and howled. Standing there, stripped to the waist, his vast beard billowing over his hairy chest, he was a grimy, angry Zeus hurling verbal thunderbolts in a crazy mixture of Spanish and English.

"Borrachos!" he roared. "Estupidos, rum-skutching borrachos! Ustedes estaban dormi-endo and let me *Queen* go on th' rocks! Why, ye poxmarked, scrovie pack o' borrachin' sea guarros! Mira! Ye swabs! Just wait till ol' Teach gits his hands on ye! I'll . . . I'll slit ever' gullet in the lot!"

His speech became garbled and incoherent. He shrieked and fired pistols at his retreating crew, but his aim was as wild as his mouthings; he hit only the sky and the water.

Lights began to flicker on the deck of the merchantman, and to gleam yellow from the windows of houses in the village. There were distant shouts of alarm. Some of the crew raced over the sand bar, raising havoc amidst swarms of sea birds; others thrashed wildly toward shore like a school of frightened tarpon.

Jonas didn't wait for more. He clawed his way up the slope. "Blackbeard," he breathed. Then he screamed, "Guards! Guards!" Soon grenadiers were swarming over the beach.

They encountered little resistance. Most of the pirates were unarmed and all of them were groggy, stunned by Blackbeard's violent and devastating attack.

Perched on the bowsprit of the *Queen Anne's Revenge,* holding aloft a bottle of rum, Edward Teach, better known as Blackbeard, greeted the oncoming longboats filled with soldiers as if they were old friends coming to visit. He was too shrewd to meet such odds with anything but jovial surrender. It was easy to fool these soldiers, fresh from England; they had heard little or nothing about Blackbeard the Pirate, terror of land and sea. To them he was nothing but a jolly seaman, a happy-go-lucky British tar.

While the soldiers wrapped yards of rope around his chest and arms, he roared with laughter. "Ye be tickling ol' Teach! He be ticklish, he is!" Deep in his chest, he chuckled. "Ain't no need for to bind up honest ol' Teach so tight! He be a gintilmin, sure and proper-like. Why, Blackbeard come for to take the Act, aims for to settle down and mend his ways, he do!"

The Act provided that if a pirate gave himself up to any one of His Majesty's colonial governors and swore to renounce his evil ways, all of his past crimes would be forgiven and he would receive a pardon. Naturally, the pirates thought highly of this ruling!

The late morning sun streamed through the windows of Governor Eden's bedroom and gleamed across a small table set with china and silver dishes containing the remnants of a hearty breakfast. Caught within a crystal decanter, it blazed scarlet in the deep purple of the Madeira wine.

Eden, in a comfortable chair, leaned back from the table, patted his round little tub of a belly, and belched. Absently, he picked up a small bell. Before the tinkling stopped, his secretary, Tobias Knight, entered the room. He extended a foot and, bending his fat body stiffly from the hips, rolled into a quick bow. "Good morning, Your Excellency, I trust you slept well?"

Eden waved his hands at an especially large chair, the only one capable of handling Knight's seating problem. "Sit down, sit down!" He smiled his mirthless smile. "I say, Tobias, tell me, do our guests find their quarters to their liking?"

"They do, Your Grace; in fact, they seem very happy about the whole thing!"

Eden was startled; his eyes bulged. "What?" he yelped. "What, what? Even with the gallows? Did not Higgins force them to build the gallows in the middle of the stockade?"

"That he did, Your Grace, but Blackbeard's taking it as nothing but a joke. He claims that he and his crew came ashore only to give themselves up and take the Act. On that basis, they are within their rights. We can't hang the scoundrels if they come in peace!" Then he added, "After all, they didn't offer any resistance."

The Governor's fat jowls went from purple to white. "Can't hang them?" he yelled. "Why, I'll hang them higher than . . . than . . ."

Tobias reached into his waistcoat pocket and removed a snuffbox. He opened it and offered it to the Governor, who angrily ignored it. Tobias took a pinch from the box, sniffed, and restored the box to his pocket. "Your Excellency," he drawled, "I had quite an interesting chat with Teach." Tobias paused and grinned slyly. "The man seems to have some very lucrative ideas . . . lucrative for Your Lordship, that is. Perhaps Your Grace might . . .?"

Eden's angry look vanished. His eyes became greedy slits. "Lucrative ideas . . . lucrative ideas?" He was a cat preparing to pounce on a mouse. "Go on, go on!"

"May I remind Your Grace that if you hang Teach you will collect only a paltry hundred pounds."

"And on the other hand," said Eden, "if I don't . . ."

Tobias grinned.

Eden went to a chair and sat. He knit his brows and pulled on his lower lip. "Hmnnn . . ." he muttered, "we really should not be too hasty in matters such as these. Perhaps it would be wise to talk to the man before we hang him. No, we must not be hasty! Never, never! It is an excellent rule — never be hasty. Yes, yes!"

Tobias hefted himself from his chair. "Begging your pardon, Your Lordship, would you care to interview the man here?"

"Yes, Tobias, here. But you go now and fetch the poor unhappy creature that we may lead him from darkness into light! Yes, that is very good . . . from darkness into light."

An hour later, Tobias hesitantly tapped on the gleaming panel of the cherrywood door. He listened for a moment, then nervously opened it. "Your Excellency," he called into the room, "I have Captain Teach. Would you . . ."

Eden's voice sounded like tin crumpling. "Teach? Teach? Send him away, you stupid fool; I have no time to see him now!"

"Yes, Your Excellency!" And Tobias backed out, bumping into the burly figure of Teach, who belly-pushed him back into the room.

"Guv'ner!" Teach roared. "Ain't got no time to lose! The quicker a body gits a ship under way the better, I always say!"

The wine in Eden's glass splashed. The goblet clinked and rattled as he placed it upon the marble-topped table. "Tobias!" he choked. "You . . . you idiot!" And with his jaws working, he watched the pirate clump to a divan and sprawl back into it, his black beard spilling over his chest.

"Guv'ner," Teach boomed. "I pats ye on the back, I does. Ye got yourself a tidy ship here!"

Eden sent a scorching look at Tobias whose

eyes were those of a whipped spaniel as he twisted his handkerchief into a tight cord.

The pirate, completely at ease, gestured broadly at the room. "Must o' cost ye a pretty penny, all this," he rumbled. "Must cost a pretty penny to keep afloat, too, I say, even on the wages of a guv'ner." He picked up a gold brocaded pillow from the sofa, gave it a pat, tossed it back, and grinned slyly at Eden. "I figures when it comes to an extra farthing, a guv'ner ain't much different than any other swab; so I figgers maybe ye'd like to hear about a little plan. It be a good 'un! It be a way ye can squeeze a little more juice out o' the guv'ner trade."

Tobias' and Eden's startled eyes met for an instant. Teach continued, and Eden slowly sank into a chair.

"It works for ye and it works for Teach . . . and it gives honest lads a living, working for Your Honor. Keep a lad busy and ye keeps him from the devil, I always say!" He eyed the decanter of wine and licked his lips; then, reaching under an armpit, he scratched vigorously.

"I can put it all in a nutshell, Guv'ner," he growled. "On dry land ye got toll roads what picks up a handsome bit. And, ye say to Blackbeard, I knows that! So I says to ye, I says, I knows ye do, and then Teach says, but does he know about that bay and river out there? *That* kin be a handsome toll road,

too . . . and it don't need no planking! All ye
needs, I say, is a fine sloop like the *Queen,*
and an honest crew o' toll collectors with a
fancy paper, writ and signed by Your Honor."

Again looks flashed between the secretary
and Eden, this time with arched eyebrows
and pursed lips.

"Thanking the Guv'ner, o' course, Blackbeard is got a honest crew, he has, what be
itching to be toll collectors." Then he added,
" 'Course I keeps the lads at Ocracoke Inlet,
what be the finest place for a water tollgate a
man ever did see!"

With the utmost dignity, Eden placed his
empty glass upon the table, clasped his fingers
across his belly, and like a well-fed bishop,
turned to Tobias. "Perhaps," he said, "our
guest would like a glass of Madeira." Then he
added, "Fill all three! We must drink to this
excellent plan . . . yes, yes, excellent plan!"

Tobias waddled to the table, filled the
glasses, picked up one and carried it to Blackbeard.

The pirate drained his glass and, holding it
against his chest, said, "Ye know, Eden, for a
time now, Teach be figgering on settling down
on shore — maybe building me a tavern for
the swabs that come in from the sea. But then
I gets to looking at them bouncing waves, and
I figgers I better build me a handsome ship,
built like no ship ever be built afore. Strong
she be . . . a ship what would last!

"But, Guv'ner, that sea out there be mighty onfriendly! Ain't no ship ever built what can stand long agin her! She gets them all, she do!

"Now the land, I say, be gentlelike, and if I be wanting something that aims to last a heap longer nor a ship, nor ol' Teach, even . . . I says to ol' Teach, I says, build yerself a dry-land house! A house strong as a ship and outen the *same kind o' wood!*

"Aye," he mused. "That I will do . . . build me a house. Maybe if honest ol' Teach stays on shore, he'll last longer too." And sheepishly grinning, he looked at Eden.

# 2

THE PLAN Teach concocted to obtain lumber to build his house was unique. A watch was kept on the bay and river for ships that were new and well built, and heaven help those who came within sight of Blackbeard. If a ship was built of mahogany or teak, and had cabins paneled in rosewood or ebony, in short order the deck of the unfortunate vessel would be teeming with pirates, followed by the ominous appearance of Teach himself.

Teach, with the nervous captain in tow, would then examine the ship from stem to stern, bewildering in his affability, making no demands for the usual toll. Instead, he would lecture with authority on the relative merits of teak and mahogany, all the while caressing sections of highly polished planking.

If Blackbeard liked what he saw, the captain of the doomed ship was politely informed that he was now in the lumber business. All Teach wanted was wood. With this request, the puzzled look on the captain's face would change to one of disbelief, followed by a complacent smile.

"Oh?" said one of these captains with a haughty smirk, "I'm afraid you picked the wrong ship! I have no lumber aboard."

"Oh yes, ye does, matey," Teach grinned. "Ye carries some o' the finest I ever did see!"

It was backbreaking labor to pry loose the teak deck, and to dislodge mahogany timbers and planking from the hull. And it wasn't easy to remove the ebony and rosewood paneling from the master's cabin, but it was done efficiently by the ship's own crew, under the direction of Blackbeard himself. The pirates, meanwhile, broke out casks of rum and made themselves comfortable, shouting advice to the hard-working seamen, with a hearty, "Heave ho, lads!" when the going got rough.

In a few months Teach had all the choice lumber he needed, and actual work on his house was begun. In the Governor's mansion, he reluctantly admitted, over a glass of Madeira, that his enterprising scheme hadn't done their toll-collection business much good. The large ships had begun to avoid the area like the plague, and collections had fallen to almost nothing. Governor Eden didn't like it, and told him so.

But at last the Boar's Head, as Teach had decided to call the tavern, was completed. The last shingle was nailed in place, the floors were waxed and polished until they gleamed like the surface of a woodland pond, and the exterior received its final coat of shining white paint. Everyone agreed it was a handsome structure.

After the last workman had left, and the mullioned windows were washed sparkling clean, Teach strutted through his dry-land home, admiring everything he saw. He pointed out details of expert workmanship to the gawking members of his crew. "Men," he boomed, "this house be built like a fine ship! We must launch her fair and properlike, with ale and rum, and the whole town to help us drink it!"

So, that very day, a special invitation was delivered to Governor Eden and his staff and a large sign was nailed to the wall of the rough log building that served as a town hall, inviting everyone to come to the grand affair. Three huge casks of ale were set up in the taproom, and there were several enormous wicker hampers containing hundreds of bottles of rum and wine. Everything was in readiness for the most lavish celebration in the history of the Carolinas! Teach and his crew of cutthroats squatted on the floor of the taproom, laughing and joking, and waited for their guests to arrive. Two hours later they were still waiting, but nobody came.

Through the open door, they could see the silent and deserted street (usually crowded with people at this time) and watch the sun, distended and red, creep downward into the purple haze above the surrounding gloom of the pine forest. By the time an uneasy messenger with a note from the Governor had arrived (and quickly left), the taproom was like a morgue. Obviously, Eden was still irked over the lost toll fees, and had sent his regrets. As for the rest of the villagers, they had locked themselves behind doors strong enough to repel an Indian attack. Within the Boar's Head, dismal and burning mad, the host and his crew sprawled on the floor, gulping rum, and waited. It was incredible that anyone could have the audacity to ignore an invitation from Blackbeard!

Finally, in the darkness of the room, Teach rose and shuffled to the open door. He stepped outside and looked up and down the dusty street. A mongrel dog sniffed its way up the street. It stopped fifty feet or so away from Teach and looked at him with wet, questioning eyes. The pirate snapped his fingers and whistled, but the animal put its head down, tail between its legs, and fled.

Blackbeard turned on his heels and stomped inside to the cask of ale, where he filled a tankard. Raising it to his lips, he drained it in one monstrous swallow, belched, and stared through the doorway, wondering why even a dog wouldn't come to his launching. He wiped his mouth with his knuckles. "Folks in this here town," he growled, "be mighty onneighborly." And, refilling his tankard, he leaned against the bar and silently glowered at the opposite wall. Then, very slowly, a grin began to work its way across Blackbeard's face, and his eyes twinkled as the ridiculous aspect of the situation struck him. He chuckled, and the chuckles grew into staccato whoops. In a few moments the whoops were roars of laughter, and the empty rooms amplified his thunder.

The crew stared in confusion at their captain, and then at each other. There were a few tentative but sheepish grins, inspired mostly by that strange infectious quality that laughter has, common to little girls, and called the giggles, which, once started, is almost impossible to stop. However, in this case there was an added reason. They were all very much aware that if Blackbeard laughed, it was unhealthy not to laugh with him, whether you got the joke or not. So, infectious mirth plus expediency in a matter of seconds had two dozen pirates rolling on the floor, howling with glee. The roars of laughter rolled from the tavern and up the darkened street to the ancient ears of the one person in town who hadn't seen or heard about the invitation to the party.

She was ugly, and bent almost double as she hobbled up the road toward the lights of the Boar's Head Tavern, a black cat slithering against the tattered folds of her skirts. She was the same old crone that Jonas Pepper had seen on the beach, and her name was Aldetha Stowecroft.

Aldetha paused in front of the tavern and listened to the howls of laughter. Her rheumy eyes sparkled as they took in the oasis of warm, lighted merriment nestled in the center of the blacked-out village. Within the taproom Teach was wiping tears of laughter from his cheeks when he saw her leering face in the window. "Aldetha!" he bawled. The face vanished. Aldetha was rapidly hobbling down the path leading to the gate. "Aldetha!" he bellowed again, but she ignored him by moving even faster. Teach caught up with her just as she reached the street.

When he re-entered the taproom a few moments later, the shy and grinning old crone was at his side, her clawlike hand curled around his arm.

"Pipe down, ye swabs!" Teach roared. "On yer feet! Whar be yer manners?"

The men scrambled to their feet and stood gawking at their skipper as he beamed down on the horrible scarecrow. She cocked her head to one side and leered up at him. He turned twinkling eyes on his men, and boomed in a voice that could be heard all over the village, "Announcing the prettiest lass in Go-dolphin Town . . . *Lady* Aldetha Stowe-croft!"

The pirates howled with delight and fell against each other in a confusion of ungainly bows. In the midst of everything, someone accidentally stepped on the cat and it screeched. Cheers and pistol shots split the warm night.

The launching went into high gear. Rum and ale flowed, bottles smashed and, within an hour, the taproom had acquired the beery smell of one twenty years older. Even if their only guests were an old woman and her cat, the party was assured of success; the bad-luck omen had been removed.

Sea chanties were roared, ballads were sung, and the men took turns dancing the hornpipe as Lady Aldetha, sitting on a keg, clapped her hands and drummed with her heels upon the barrel. That night, for the first time in more than forty years, Aldetha Stowe-croft received something from her fellow man besides scorn, fear, and abuse.

From that day on, she never left the Boar's Head, but was given the position of house-keeper. Aldetha Stowecroft had found a home at last and, along with her cat became as much a part of the place as the stone fireplace and the mahogany floors. Not only did she keep the rooms spick-and-span, but during those long periods when Teach and his crew were at sea, Aldetha was constantly on guard against anyone who might molest that which was Blackbeard's. In this capacity, she and her cat were worth more than a dozen watchdogs.

So the grand "launching" was a success after all and Lady Aldetha Stowecroft wound up the most glorious night of her life by falling asleep curled up under the bar with Diablo purring contentedly at her side.

Following the launching, peace reigned in Godolphin. But it was just too good to last. The Governor and the pirates had grown wealthy, but the townspeople became poorer because without shipping, business comes to a standstill, and Godolphin had once more become a port honest sea captains avoided. By the time the scrub oaks were blazing red and gold, the citizens had had enough. Secretly, a committee was selected which paid a call on Governor Spotswood of Virginia. The Governor told them that, although he couldn't do anything about Governor Eden, he could and would do something about Blackbeard and his crew. The group of men returned to Godolphin Town and waited hopefully.

On the 15th of November, 1718, Blackbeard told Aldetha to keep a sharp eye on things. "I be a-going," he said, "to Ocracoke Inlet for a spell. . . . I aims to do a bit o' courting, I do." He grinned and winked. "Don't ye be startled none effen ol' Teach brings back a bride this here trip!" Aldetha would not have been startled in the least.

Teach stroked Diablo's sleek coat and gave
Aldetha a friendly pat. Then, hitching up his
belt, he clumped from the house and headed
for the harbor.

Two heavily armed sloops were sailing south
from Hampton Roads. Captain Brand was in
command of one, and Lieutenant Robert Maynard the other. Their orders: capture Blackbeard and his crew or rid the sea of him. Both
men had their eyes on that one hundred
pounds reward that Eden had not bothered
to collect. One hundred pounds was an enormous amount of money.

On November 21, they sighted the *Queen
Anne's Revenge* lying at anchor at Ocracoke.
Teach saw the ships and knew who they were.
He had no respect for young officers and he
made no attempt to escape. Actually, Blackbeard was eager for a savage sea battle. The
long, peaceful summer had been boring, and
collecting toll a monotonous pastime. Maynard's sloop, the *Pearl,* grated alongside the
*Revenge* and instantly Teach and his crew
swarmed aboard her, thinking they had an
easy victory. But, for once, Blackbeard was
outsmarted. From the hold and other places of
concealment leaped dozens of British seamen,
and the pirates were overwhelmed — all except Blackbeard.

Covered with blood from more than twenty
wounds, he hacked his way toward Lieutenant
Maynard. Both drew pistols and fired. Blackbeard's ball whined harmlessly, but Maynard's

struck Teach in the face. Immediately, his
beard was drenched with blood and, screeching
with rage, he slashed at the young lieutenant
with his cutlass. Steel clashed as Maynard
fought back, thrusting with his light naval
sword. One of Maynard's men closed in on
Teach from the side; his cutlass sliced a
screaming arc, striking Teach on the neck and
almost decapitating him.

With his hand, Blackbeard held his head in
place, spun around and drove his cutlass
through the seaman. Then, roaring, he backed
against a mast. Several bullets plowed through
his body. He aimed his pistol at Maynard, but
before he could pull the trigger, his eyes
glazed and it dropped from his lifeless fingers.
Dead on his feet, he did not fall but remained
propped against the mast on widespread legs,
his dead eyes staring at Maynard.

The ship lurched, and the body of Edward
"Blackbeard" Teach slowly crashed to the
deck.

Lieutenant Robert Maynard collected his
hundred pounds reward and Governor Eden,
not intending to be outdone by Spotswood,
and at the same time proving he was on the
side of law and order, presented him with the
Boar's Head Tavern.

Aldetha Stowecroft was convicted of witchcraft, and on the sixth day of January, 1719,
she was burned at the stake.

# 1: FRIDAY AND SATURDAY

## 3

ON A FRIDAY AFTERNOON in the spring, two
boys shouldered through the slow-moving mass
of students blocking the entrance of Godolphin Junior High. They plowed between chattering teenagers and headed rapidly in the
direction of Main Street and Maynard Avenue
and the Boar's Head Tavern.

The two fourteen-year-old boys had slowed
their run to a walk when the one who was tall,
lanky, and freckled spoke. "They ain't really
going to tear down the Boar's Head, are they,
J.D.?"

" 'Course they are . . . they've already
started," replied J.D., who was dark and stocky.

"Heck! That will louse up everything! Why

does anyone want to tear down a perfectly good haunted house?"

" 'Cause that old crab Joe Maynard finally sold the land for a gas station," said J.D., "that's why. Come on," he added impatiently, "let's get going! They'll have the place torn down before we get there!"

From within the Boar's Head Tavern could be heard the erratic hollow thump of pounding hammers, and the crash and rattle of falling plaster. Jake Kowalek, a gaunt man of about sixty, was the foreman of the demolition gang. Right now, Jake had a look of baffled worry on his face as he blew a lazy cloud of tobacco smoke in the direction of the roof of the old building.

He walked across the rubble-strewn floor of what once had been the main room in the house, the taproom, and ducked under a long doorway that opened into a long, narrow room with a low ceiling. Here most of the plaster and lath had been removed, exposing gigantic beams.

Two dusty workmen stood facing each other. One of them had his head tilted to one side and his mouth wide open as he faced the window, while the other, using a bandanna handkerchief, was trying to remove a particle of plaster from his eye. "Hold still, will ya," he complained. "How can I get it out if ya keep jumping around?"

The foreman looked carefully into the teary

eye. He put his hand on the injured man's shoulder. "Look, Jerry, it ain't too bad, but you better take that eye to a pro. Let Doc Rolls have a look at it." Am I nuts? he thought. That's the sixth guy I'm losing in one day! Six jokers with stupid injuries, just bad enough to make them useless for anything except to go home and watch baseball on TV. This casualty business was getting out of hand! Who was the dope that built this place, anyway? There's hardly a nail in the place — all pegs and dowels, and nothing wants to come loose! And the hammer heads that keep flying off, and everybody getting sore at everybody else . . . and now Jerry, my best man, gets something in his eye and I lose him! I'll bet a plugged nickel he won't be back for two days.

The job at the start had been a simple one. All the later additions to the tavern were easily pulled down and hauled away, especially all that fancy gingerbread stuff. But now that they were down to what his boss, Mr. Bailly, said was "Early American," they were getting into one mess after another. Well, the time had come to throw it back in Mr. Bailly's lap. Muttering to himself, Jake strode across the street to the corner drugstore and a telephone. He dropped a coin into the slot and dialed. He waited, absently studying the ceiling.

"Good afternoon, Summit Oil Company," chirped a feminine voice into his hairy ear.

"Hello," he said, "is Bailly in, Alice?"

"Who shall I say is calling?"

"It's me — Jake! Lemme talk to Bailly."

J.M. Bailly's voice was the grating roar of coal being poured through the tailgate of a truck. Jake winced and moved the receiver three inches from his ear.

"All right," Bailly growled, "so what's bugging you now?"

"Plenty, boss. I know this stuff I'm going to tell you will sound crazy, but it's true. Nothing in that stupid shack will come loose; it's put together like a jigsaw puzzle! I had to lay off six guys on account of injuries, and some wise guy keeps hiding the lunch boxes . . ."

"Is *that* all?"

"Heck, no!" Jake retorted. "Tools disappear, and you know that brand new air hammer we got? Well, it either won't work at all, or when it does, it jumps around like a snake so nobody can hang on to the blamed thing! It chased Mac right out of the house! Then a little while ago the place was filled up with smoke that stunk to high heaven."

"A fire?"

"No, it wasn't a fire, boss, just stinking smoke, like from garbage burning, then it went away like magic! Drove everybody off the job for an hour."

Jake waited for his boss to comment. When he didn't, Jake continued. "Another thing. One of the boys found a dungeon way down under the place; it's like a jail — cells, rings in the walls, the works. Spookier than the dickens! Well, that's the kind of crud we been running into all along, boss. What do you suppose we ought to do about that crazy place! Some of the guys are griping because they say it's haunted!"

Jake waited for a reply. Then he said, "Boss . . . ? Boss . . . ?" Jake removed the receiver from his ear, looked at it quizically, then put it back and shouted, "*BOSS!*"

"Shut up, you loud-mouthed fool!" Bailly yelled. "You want to break my eardrum?"

Jake scowled. "I thought we was cut off . . ." Then he said, "What do you think we ought to do about that place?"

"Look, chum," Bailly snarled. "I've got news for you! Your job is to get that shack out of the way, and *fast!* If you couldn't get it out of the way by tearing it down, why didn't you accidentally drop a match somewheres?"

Jake grinned fiendishly and said, "You wouldn't want me to do *that*, Mr. Bailly!"

"Why?"

Jay chuckled. "You know all them big beams and timbers that must've come from a ship?"

"Yeah, so what?"

"All of them, in fact every goldurned stick of wood in that house is either mahogany, chestnut, or teak, and there's a lot of rosewood, and stuff I don't even know the name of. I tell you the place is a wooden gold mine!

The trouble is, you can't take it apart! I started a couple of men ripping off shingles . . . sure, the top ones came off real easylike, but the original ones, down underneath . . . ha! You just try and get them loose!"

"Why can't you get them loose?"

"You tell me, boss!"

"Hmmmnn," said Bailly; then he added, "What are they made of, gold?"

Jake, for the first time, was really enjoying a talk with his boss.

"Uh-uh," came his grinning and negative answer, "not such cheap stuff as that. Them shingles are made of ebony!"

"Ebony!" Bailly gasped. "Ebony! Who could have been so stinking rich or so stupid as to put ebony shingles on the roof of a house?"

"The guy that built the place was. I guess he wanted it to last forever. And for my money, the way it's going, it will!"

Again there was dead silence.

"Boss . . . *Boss!*"

There came no response. Bailly was lost in a maze of mahogany, haunted houses, rosewood, fat profits, ebony, and ghosts. Mostly ghosts. When he finally spoke, the coal chute delivered soft, smooth sand. "Yeah," he said weakly, "I'm listening."

"What about the men? I think we ought to let them knock off for the day, with pay. If we don't, I don't think a single man will show

on Monday. . . . Believe me, those boys have
had it!" Jake paused, then added, "It's close to
quitting time. . . ."

"Okay."

"What about you, Mr. Bailly? Could you
take a run over here? You should take a look
at this stuff . . . that is, if the smoke and
stink is gone!"

"I'd like to, Jake, but I'm going out of town.
I've got to catch a plane in an hour."

"Oh."

"I'll be back by noon on Monday . . .
maybe a little later. You better hold things up
until I get there. I'll see you then, Jake."

"Okay, boss."

Baily hung up the phone and sank wearily
back into his ultramodern swivel chair. His
face was still gray. He pinched his full lower
lip thoughtfully and stared at the telephone.
"Ebony!" he muttered to himself. "Solid ebony
shingles!"

# 4

J. D. Jones and Hank Oberteuffer watched the crew of workmen grudgingly enter the house and then quickly reappear bearing tools and other equipment, which they dumped into the truck before climbing aboard. With Jake at the wheel, the engine sputtered into a roar and the truck began moving slowly forward. It followed a bumpy and winding route through the grass between the elms and, after passing through an opening in the fence, entered the street. The Boar's Head Tavern was deserted and the grounds about it were like a neglected and forsaken picnic grove. The bystanders had gone, leaving J.D. and Hank the only ones still interested in the tragic fate of the old tavern.

Hank looked at J.D. and J.D. looked at Hank. Then, without a word, both boys darted through the gate, up the path, and into the taproom of the Boar's Head. They ranged from room to room, exploring and inspecting everything. They noticed that some of the partitions had been removed; things were different.

With the flimsy additions of later years stripped away, revealing the hand-hewn timbers and the rough yellowed plaster of the original construction, the rooms appeared to be far more ancient and venerable, but the ghostly look was magnified. More than ever the interior of the Boar's Head was an eerie stage where apparition and specter roamed, playing their dismal roles.

Hank picked up a *genuine* antique, a four-inch length of tallow candle that, by some miracle, had not been devoured by rats or mice. He put it into his pocket.

J.D. was the first to speak. "Sort of looks different, don't it?"

"Yeah," said Hank.

"The only stuff they tore out was stuff that was built on afterwards. Now it's just like it was when Blackbeard lived here." J.D. walked away from Hank and began snooping between some exposed timbers. Hank watched, wondering what J.D. was looking for.

"Yaaa . . ." he sneered. "How do you know all that junk?"

J.D. was Hank's best friend, and they were

inseparable, but J.D. irritated Hank quite often when he told him things that Hank didn't know. These occasions occurred more often than he would admit to J.D., or even to himself!

"How do I know what?" J.D. mumbled.

"That stuff you said about this house and about Blackbeard. How do *you* know he lived here?" Hank poked his head into an adjoining space between the timbers and repeated the question. "Who told *you* that Blackbeard used to live in this house?" He liked the way his voice sounded; it was strange and echoed hollowly.

J.D. was emphatic. "I *always* knew *that!* And I heard about the house being back the way it was from some people who were talking about it on the sidewalk out there. Didn't you hear them? And holy cow! Didn't you know that Blackbeard the Pirate *built* this place?"

" 'Course I did," Hank lied. "Think I'm stupid?" He watched J.D. sift plaster rubble between his fingers. "What you looking for in here?"

"Old junk," said J.D., backing out and rising to his feet. "Pop Allan told me you can find a lot of valuable stuff in an old house like this when they tear it down." He walked along the wall, peering into various apertures.

"No kidding!" said Hank, very much impressed. He withdrew his head and dropped to his knees, squeezing his shoulders into the same area J.D. had just vacated. Only his skinny bottom protruded. He searched the rubble diligently, without success. "I don't see nothing, J.D.," he complained.

"Just keep looking."

After a silence of about three minutes, Hank suddenly yelped, "Hey, J.D., look!" and scrambled from between the timbers. He sat on the floor, intently scrutinizing his find. It was a bright yellow disc-shaped object about the size of a silver dollar.

"What did you find?"

"This!"

J.D. hurried across the room and squatted beside his friend.

"It's a funny-looking medal," said Hank and handed it to J.D., who rose to his feet and carried it to a window where there was more light. Hank followed. J.D.'s eyes were filled with envy. "Golly!" he breathed. "Where did you find this?" Hank grinned his triumph. Then, with affected nonchalance, he said, "Over there, in the place where you were looking."

"Boy! Are *you* lucky!' murmured J.D.

"What do you suppose it is, some kind of a medal?"

"Uh-uh," J.D. grunted. "It's money . . . real old money," He looked at Hank. "You wanna know something? I think this here coin is old Spanish money like a piece-of-eight, or a doubloon, and it's *real gold!* We can ask

Pop Allan, he'll know. You realize, Hank, Blackbeard himself might have owned this?"

To say that Hank snatched the coin from J.D. wouldn't be exactly true, but it was almost true. "Let me see that thing," he gulped. "Jeepers! Maybe the place is loaded with 'em!"

By the time Hank had carefully pushed the gold coin deep into the bottom of his pocket, J.D. was on his hands and knees between the walls, absorbed in an enthusiastic search for hidden treasure.

"Think there's any more of them, J.D.?" asked Hank, his hand reaching blindly under some floor boards.

"What?" came J.D.'s entombed voice. "I didn't hear you."

Hank shouted this time. "I said do you think we can find any more of them gold coins?"

"Could be."

They worked like hungry moles, digging and sifting through plaster dust and rubble, peering into crannies, minutely examining hidden places unseen by human eye for over two centuries. They painfully squeezed into nooks the workmen had made accessible by ripping away sheathing and Victorian wainscoting, and grubbed their way across two hundred and fifty years of accumulated dust and spiderwebs.

After an hour of toil, Hank had discovered: one rusty thimble, a brass key (not very old), one greasy spark plug, and six hand-forged nails (four of them twisted and bent). J.D. fared even worse. The only thing he could find was a matchbook of recent vintage with four matches missing. Printed in bold red type on the cover was HARRY'S ELITE DINER, while on the back, letters of gold proclaimed, *"We cook like ma . . . just ask pa!"* The matches were in excellent condition, and J.D. kept them.

Hank was the first to tire and lose his enthusiasm for the recovery of long-lost treasures. He gave up the search and peered in between the beams at J.D., who was crawling on his belly, enveloped in a fog of plaster dust, fruitlessly scrounging deeper and deeper into dark and mysterious places. "I tell you, J.D., you ain't gonna find anything. Why don't you quit?" With this uninspiring comment, Hank left J.D. to his labors and entered the long, dismal spider-webbed hallway which led to the taproom.

J.D. acted as if he had not heard, but continued in his diligent quest for a coin — any kind of coin! The tall and lanky boy had been gone from the room only a few minutes when J.D. heard his startled yell.

"Jeepers! J.D., c'mere, quick!"

A very dirty J.D. was slapping dust from his jeans when an even dirtier Hank made an excited, arm-waving entrance. Under his nose was a black smear that looked like an off-center Groucho Marx mustache. His green eyes were snapping with excitement, and his words were almost incoherent as they tumbled from his lips. "Wait till you see what I found! Man, this is really something!"

J.D. gave him a vague look. "Yeah," he said, and went back to his brushing. Although inwardly burning with curiosity, he didn't hurry the dry-cleaning operation.

"Aw, forget that, J.D.," Hank urged. "C'mon, you got to see this!"

"Okay," J.D. said in a tired kind of way, trying his best to sound bored. He followed Hank up the corridor with all the indifference he could muster. Halfway, he forced himself to stop and check a shoelace that needed no attention. Hank was fidgety, squirming, a picture of impatience as he stood framed in the doorway to the taproom and watched the seemingly endless shoelace ritual. "Aw, c'mon," he groaned. "Jeepers, that can wait!"

As Hank fumed, J.D. had a most disturbing vision. His friend was kneeling gleefully beside an ancient pirate treasure chest. It was filled to the brim with doubloons of bright and shining gold, and he, J.D. Jones, had to stand there, fat, dumb and empty-handed, watching the super-lucky Hank dig his grubby hands into the golden hoard, letting a million doubloons trickle through his fingers.

With this vision uppermost in his mind, J.D. drearily rose to his feet. He had convinced himself that Hank had really found something extremely valuable and, fearing the worst, was afraid to ask what it was. With these gloomy thoughts, he shuffled toward Hank and the doorway. "Awright," he said, "what did you find that's so great?"

"A doorway!"

"A *doorway?*" J.D. yelled with mingled surprise and relief. "Is that all?"

"Sure . . . but wait'll you see it!"

J.D. Jones once more became the real J.D. Jones — exuberant, superior, confident, a wide grin on his round face. "You mean all you found was a ol' doorway, and you get all steamed up over it? Are you kidding? I know every doorway in this shack!"

"Oh yeah? Well, you don't know about this one," said Hank angrily. He moved toward some planks stacked like a lean-to against the taproom wall. He pointed to the lumber and spoke in a voice tinctured with indignation and hurt. "Okay, wise guy, if you don't want to believe me! Take a look for yourself; it's right in back of this junk!"

With that blast of indignation off his chest, Hank dropped to his knees and squirmed into the space between the planks and the wall.

What was Hank trying to hand him, anyhow? This outburst was pretty convincing but it didn't make sense. Hank never *ever* pulled gags or played jokes on anyone. So, maybe he wants to start now, and this is his idea of a gag! There *couldn't* be a doorway in that wall. If there was, how did it get there all of a sudden? "I'll be doggoned if I'll bite on this stupid gag," J.D. muttered.

But Hank's voice was filled with sincerity and urgency. "Hurry up, J.D., you gotta see this; it's terrific!" J.D. went to the place where Hank had squeezed under the planks, wiggled his way into an area that resembled the interior of a small shed. Hank greeted him with a wide, victorious grin.

"See?" he chortled. "What did I tell you? I told you there was a doorway in this place you never knew about!"

J.D. stared through the open doorway, and his eyes widened. He breathed two astonished words, "Holy cow!" Then, following Hank, he scrambled to the remarkable entrance. Both knelt on the doorstep and peered down into a gloomy, dark circular stairwell. They saw walls, steps, and ceiling built of smooth, carefully laid stone, splotched with a sickening gray-green mold. They saw ancient spiderwebs, thick with dust, hanging from the walls and ceiling like miniature torn and shredded velvet shrouds. It was musty and damp and smelled like a tomb, and from the depths came a steady draft of clammy air. From far below, they could hear the constant, drip, drip of water.

"Wow!" marveled J.D. "This musta been Blackbeard's secret doorway."

"I bet you're right," said Hank. Then he added with an I-told-you-so smirk, "Next time, I guess you'll believe me when I tell you something about something!"

Ignoring the remark, J.D. got to his feet,

stooping to avoid the planking. "I wonder where it leads to," he mused, taking the first step down the ghostly stairway.

"Yeah, so do I," said Hank vacantly. Then he gasped and scrambled to his feet also. "Hey! Are you going down there?"

"Sure, why not? Ain't you?"

"Heck, no!"

A slow mocking grin drifted across J.D.'s face. "Now, look, Hank, don't tell me you're *scared* all of a sudden!"

Hank's explosive reply was more in the nature of a challenge than a question. "Who's scared!"

"Well, okay then, if you ain't scared, let's go down there and see what it's like."

With a great show of bravado, Hank pushed his way past J.D. Four steps down he stopped and scowled down into the gloom. "Just the way I figgered," he said, and quickly clumped back up the stairs.

"What?" asked J.D.

"It's so dark down there you wouldn't be able to see a darn thing!"

"You got a candle, I got matches!"

Hank now wished fervently that he hadn't found the old candle, and that he hadn't discovered the old doorway and the steps. He wasn't scared; he was just careful! He didn't like dark places, anyway. He never had. J.D. was a nice guy, the best friend he ever had, but J.D. was always putting a guy on the spot — always thinking up crazy things to do, like this one, for instance. Why did some people always have to go around sticking their noses into things, trying to find out about stuff, the way J.D. did all the time?

Reluctantly he dug into his pocket and withdrew the candle, and then checked another pocket to be sure the gold coin was still there. "It won't work; it's too old," he said, holding the thick, round stump of yellow tallow out to J.D., all the while hoping that he was right.

J.D. was eagerly waiting, matchbook in one hand and a match ready to strike in the other. "No," he said, "you hold the candle; I'll light it." The match tip burst into flame and J.D. held it under the candle wick. Tiny sparks, like shooting stars, crackled and leaped. Then, after two hundred years of darkness and cold, the candle spluttered into hot, blazing life. It didn't have the mellow, clean flame of a modern wax candle. This one smoked and burned the way tarpaper does, with a sulphurous, sickly flame. It guttered and smelled of burning fat, glowing bright, then dim, then blazing bright again. It blackened the shadows, and made them come ominously alive.

One look at the sputtering flame convinced Hank that this could be far worse than no light at all, and he eyed it with dismay, "Ain't very good, is it?"

"No," agreed J.D., as he took the candle from Hank's hand, "but it works."

Hank swiped at his nose with the back of his wrist, snuffled, and eyed the downward-curving steps beyond J.D.'s feet. "Look," he said, "I'll get my flashlight. That's a crummy candle; it'll go out for sure!"

"No, it won't, Hank. It's working pretty good." J.D. paused, then said, "Hey, wait a minute! You don't think I'm going all the way down there! I'm only going down a few steps."

Hank frowned. "But look, J.D. It'd only take me a couple of seconds to get my flashlight. My dad got new batteries. It really works now."

"So — okay, but you know what'll happen if you go home. Your mother will think up something for you to do, and I'll be stuck here waiting!" He paused, then he pleaded, "I don't wanta go down in there alone, Hank. The candle will be all right!" His brown eyes begged with an irresistible pleading look that reminded Hank of his dog Butch.

J.D.'s warning about running into a flock of errands and chores was almost as convincing as the request for moral support. Pleas of this kind by anyone, and especially by J.D., was rare. Hank felt important, intensely flattered, and somewhat cocky.

"C'mon, Hank! Let's go!" J.D. pleaded. As it commonly does, enthusiasm, plus logic, plus flattery, won, and Hank, as always, ended up by doing exactly what J.D. wanted him to do.

# 5

THE STAIRS wound steeply downward. Hank followed close behind J.D., one hand on his friend's shoulder, the other slipping over the cold, smooth stones, seeking additional support. In silence the boys descended; the street noises gradually faded away. Now, except for the sound of water dripping, the silence was deadly. It was like a soggy blanket.

Suddenly Hank shrieked as if he had gone mad. He frantically slapped his chest and the back of his neck. He twisted about, writhed, and stamped his feet. He hadn't seen the dusty cobweb on the wall, and his hand had sloughed through it! Something black with several legs had landed on his wrist and scurried up his arm into the short, loose sleeve of his T-shirt.

"Golly, Hank, what's the matter? You nearly made me drop the candle!"

"Jeepers," grasped Hank, "a spider or something awful crawled up my arm! C'mon, let's get out of here!"

"Is it gone?"

"Yeah, I think so."

"Well, forget it, then."

"Oh, no! I'm leaving," Hank announced flatly in a tone that indicated no ifs, ands, or buts. J.D., on the verge of admitting defeat, sent a last disappointed glance downward.

"Wait a second, Hank!" he yelped. "Look!"

"Huh?" said Hank, turning back.

"I was just going to tell you, but then you let out that awful yell. Look down there!"

"Where?" asked Hank, taking a step downward. "I don't see nothing."

"Right there!" J.D. shielded the flame and nodded his head in the direction of the lower steps.

"How do you suppose daylight gets down here, J.D.?"

"Golly, I don't know. How deep do you think we are?"

J.D. didn't wait for Hank's reply; he impetuously surged ahead.

"Hey! Where are you going with that candle? How d'ya expect me to see?"

The candle wasn't needed any more and Hank continued his cautious descent, all the while voicing his indignant opinion of people who ran off with candles in dark stairwells. He heard the rhythmic pound of J.D.'s feet abruptly change cadence and flounder into violent scraping sounds, ending in a dull thud and a muffled "Oomph!"

"Jeepers!" Hank gasped. Now, except for the distant moan of a dying siren and the drip of water, there was silence. "J.D.!" he screamed and clattered down the stairwell. To gain momentum, he curled his hands around the center post and careened down the stairs like the end player in a game of crack-the-whip.

J.D. heard him coming. "Watch out for the step!" he shouted, and his voice reverberated, but the warning came too late, and Hank duplicated J.D.'s violent tumble into Blackbeard's secret dungeon. He slammed into J.D., who was trying to scramble out of the way, and both boys rolled across the floor in a tangle of arms and legs.

J.D. was the first to extricate himself. He stood and looked down at Hank, who was sitting on the floor vacantly rubbing his elbow. "Holy cow!" he exploded. "Didn't you hear me holler for you to watch out for that trip step?"

Hank's eyes gradually came into focus. He rubbed his elbow and balefully stared at the evil step. "Criminy! What a stupid way to have a step!"

"It ain't stupid."

Hank turned in amazement and stared at J.D., who was contemplating the ceiling. "What do you mean, it ain't stupid? They got one of them steps twice as high as all the rest of them! You mean to stand there and tell me that ain't stupid?" Then he added scornfully, "'Course maybe you *like* falling downstairs!"

"I wouldn't have, if I lived here and knew about it!" J.D. replied indignantly. He turned and pointed at the step. "That's called a trip step — a lot of old castles in Europe had them."

"Trip step!" Hank exclaimed. "How dumb can you get! They must have been awful crazy back in those days. Did they actually *want* to break their necks every time they went down a goofy flight of stairs?" He shuffled toward the bottom of the stairwell and examined the sixth step. The riser was twice as high as any of the others.

"Look," said J.D., "what if you were living in this house back in those days, and some creep with a long knife came after you and chased you down those stairs? You know about the step, of course, but he don't. So okay, what happens? He ends up on his ear, but you don't. You're okay and waiting at the bottom with a club or something. Those joes back then weren't so dumb!"

He turned away and left Hank squinting at the step as if he were seeing it for the first time. The dim light came from a shaft which led to the surface, and J.D. began nosing about in the recesses of the dungeon, where some heavy iron chains had been fastened to rings in the wall. They were dusty and dust-covered; at the end of each was a small iron collar.

"Golly, Hank. Wait'll we tell Pop Allan about this place; he'll flip." J.D. nudged the chains with his foot. "These must've been the leg irons that they used for the prisoners — you know, people Blackbeard was holding for ransom and stuff like that." Eagerly, J.D. took off and rapidly clumped over the rubble-strewn floor toward three low, narrow doorways located in the most distant and dismal part of the dungeon. He gaped at the heavy, ponderous doors which effectively and ominously blocked two of these entranceways. The enormous hinges of the third, which was closest to the shaft, had long ago rusted away and the door had collapsed. Each door had a monstrous padlock and, near the top, a small square opening covered with iron grillwork. They were rust-pocked with decay, and seemed to be welded to the surrounding stone wall with dust-thickened cobwebs.

J.D. turned in the direction of Hank, who was closely investigating the chains and the floor beneath them, another gleaming gold doubloon in the back of his mind. "C'mere," J.D. urgently exclaimed, "take a look . . . this was a prison cell!"

By the time Hank had moved across the stone floor to the cell, J.D. had stepped into the tiny room. The light from the shaft, which softly illuminated the area, revealed there was nothing much to see except a low-arched ceiling and walls built of rough stone. In one corner, where the mortar had crumbled, a stone had fallen from the wall, leaving a black, gaping emptiness. Gingerly, J.D. put his hand into the hole. His fingers closed around something that felt like a dead rat's dried skin. He forced himself to draw out the horrid thing and was relieved to find it was only a dusty roll of paper.

"Hey, Hank, look what I got," he shouted in triumph. He carefully unrolled the stiff, crackly paper as Hank moved toward the door. "Okay, so you got a stupid piece of paper. Now let's go," said Hank impatiently.

"There's some kind of writing on it. Holy cow, Hank, is this ever old!" J.D. hurriedly squeezed by his friend on his way out of the cell and headed toward the shaft of light.

"Yeah?" said Hank. "What's it say?"

Under the light, J.D. studied the paper closely. "I don't know . . . it ain't very plain." He felt the texture, tried to fold it, inspected it curiously on both sides. "You know, this isn't paper; it's that kind of stuff they print diplomas on. I think it's called parchment."

Unnoticed by the two friends, the dungeon had been growing gloomier, and suddenly the branches of the elms above the ventilating shaft thrashed about in the wind of a spring storm. Lightning flashed, and there was the distant rumble of thunder. Hank looked up the shaft at the circle of darkening sky, wondering why he had let J.D. talk him into coming down here. Why did he always let J.D. talk him into everything? Boy, he thought, am I a stupid jerk! Then he turned to J.D. and said nervously, "So, okay, it's parchment. Let's get out of here. It's going to rain any minute."

At this, a cat appeared in the entrance to the cell, stared balefully at the boys, and from this sleek, black bundle of ferocity came an earsplitting, almost human cry of what sounded like elation. Startled, both boys shot a frightened look at the cat. Then came a deafening crash of thunder and the tomblike chamber became even colder. Hank shivered. "Golly, did you ever see such a spooky cat?"

The tomcat eyed them, arching his back. His malevolent hiss revealed long white fangs. He sprang from the doorway and, like a smear of black shadow, streaked between the boys across the chamber, up the steps, and was gone.

"Wow!" Hank exploded. "I'm getting out of here!"

"Look up there, you lug. Can't you see it's started to rain?" J.D. turned back to the yellowed parchment, holding it in the light but away from the drops of rain that now fell through the shaft. Hank looked longingly at the dungeon stairwell where the cat had made his dramatic exit. "We could at least go upstairs," he said.

"Why?" asked J.D.

Then Hank's interest in the paper caused his curiosity to win again, and he, too, turned to scrutinize the document over his friend's shoulder, his freckled face screwed up in puzzled concentration.

"Can you make out what it says, J.D.?"

J.D. sniffed and rubbed his nose with the back of his hand. "I think so."

The ink had faded to the color of old, dried blood, and the legend was written in a curious, almost illegible script, followed by a group of cabalistic symbols and strange diagrams. J.D. read laboriously. "It says, 'These be the words and marks of Satan.' "

"Aw," Hank scoffed, "what are you trying to hand me?"

"Okay, wise guy, read it yourself!"

Hank studied the parchment more closely, then he gulped, stared at it as if it were a poisonous snake, and backed away. "Jeepers," he said slowly, "better we put it back, huh? I think we oughta forget about it."

Ignoring these words of wisdom, and without taking his eyes from the document, J.D. moved closer to the light. He read silently, now and then muttering an astonished "Holy cow!"

"Well, criminy, J.D., you could at least read it out loud!"

J.D. rubbed his nose again. "It says, 'O speak these words of black magic and bring ye curse of Satan to . . .' " He looked up. "The next stuff is so blurry I can't make it out. Could be Eden and Robert May . . . something like that." He squinted and held the parchment closer to his nose. "Then it says, 'Writ in my own true blood, ye day I burn at stake,' and it's signed, Lady Aldetha Stowecroft, January sixth, seventeen . . . looks like 1719, or something. It's smeary, like with bloodstains. Then the rest is just a bunch of crazy words."

Suddenly his eyes blazed with excitement. "Holy cow, Hank, you know what that *is?*"

"Uh-uh, what?"

"It's old witchcraft stuff! You know, black magic!"

J.D. walked rapidly toward the cell, then spun around to face Hank, waving the scroll. "Don't you remember in Social Studies last year, Pop Allan was telling about how, back in the old days, they burned some witches around here?"

There was a blank look on Hank's face.

"Sure!" J.D. went on, enthused. "Don't you remember about how they burned those people because someone said they was a witch?"

"Oh yeah, now I remember," said Hank slowly.

"Sure! Some old witch must have written this, and I bet it's been stuck in that wall over two hundred years!"

"No kidding!" Hank rose from the steps, went to J.D.'s side, and looked with new interest at the scroll.

J.D. tapped with his forefinger on the words,

his face bright with new inspiration. "This here is our answer!"

Hank's face again went blank. "Answer? Answer to what?"

"To make some money, you lug! We can put on a seance!"

"A say-ance? What the heck is a say-ance?"

J.D.'s face screwed up in pained surprise. "You mean you ain't never heard of a seance?"

Hank shook his head. "Uh-uh." He pointed at the scroll. "What's *that* got to do with it?"

"Why, just everything, that's all!" J.D., with much care, rolled up the parchment and, setting the scene with his hands, began. "It's all dark, see, and a guy goes into a trance and starts talking in a real spooky voice to the spirits and stuff . . ."

Hank's look of alarm was disregarded as J.D. continued enthusiastically. "Then they come drifting in . . ."

"Who comes drifting in?"

"The ghosts, of course!"

"Real ghosts? You're kidding!"

"Of course not real ghosts, but the people watching *think* they're real. Now, shut up, will you? You want to hear about it?"

"Okay."

"They come drifting in and make weird noises, and all that junk." He looked down at the scroll as Hank eyed him fearfully. "Let's do it, Hank! You know how the kids like ghost stories. This will be even better! Just think of the money we'll make!" He poked

the scroll at Hank, who backed up so hastily
he almost tripped over a mammoth chain fastened to the wall. "We can use some of my old
magic tricks in a different way . . . you
know, like the one where I make a piece of
cloth raise up by itself?"

"I don't know," said Hank warily, keeping
his eyes on the scroll and backing nervously
toward the stairs. "What if a real ghost shows
up? Then what?"

There came another crash of thunder, very
close this time, and Hank winced. J.D. kicked
a small rock across the dungeon floor in disgust, and said scornfully, "You don't actually
believe all that stuff, do you? It won't really
work, stupid! Even in a *real* seance the stuff is
all phony! My dad said so. It's nothing but a
bunch of tricks, just like we been doing in
those magic shows we put on, a lot of Halloween stuff!"

"Well," said Hank, only partially convinced,
"I don't know."

Now the cat, looking half drowned, reappeared on the steps. His eyes glared and from
his throat came a loud, unearthly growl of pure
hatred. Hank shrank back against the damp,
cold wall.

"Scat!" shouted J.D., as he tossed a handful
of rubble in the direction of the cat, who made
no move, but spat once more in his vicious,
defiant manner, then turned and silently vanished again.

"I wish that cat would stay out of here,"

said Hank. "This place is bad enough as it is. I hate cats anyhow!"

"Aw, forget it," drawled J.D. "Let's talk about the seance idea." He walked to the light, avoiding the rain and the little streams of water that were now dripping from the sides of the shaft and forming puddles between the flagstones. He stood looking upward, contemplating the rain. Impulsively, he spun about.

"Hey! You know what, Hank?" We could fix a table so it raises by itself, like a ghost was doing it! And we could use this stuff . . . the magic words and everything!"

Hank stared at him aghast. "Are you crazy?" he blurted. "Look, you aren't going to use *that,* are you? If you do, you can count me out!" He pointed to the scroll. "What if that stuff was written by a real witch? What if we try it and it really works? Then what?"

"Holy cow, Hank, we've *got* to use it! Do you want to spoil everything? There's a lot of scary stuff in it!" Quickly he added, "Of course, it doesn't mean anything. It's just a bunch of crazy words and pictures like a kid would draw. And look, I *told* you my dad said all that ghost business was phony! And he ought to know. He was at a real seance, and so was my mother."

"Did your mother say it was all phony too?"

"Well, no, not exactly . . . she said . . ."

"*My* dad said this place is haunted, and he oughta know as well as *your* dad. Old sourpuss Maynard had him fix the plumbing in here once, and no matter what he did, it just kept breaking down again!"

"Holy cow, Hank, what has plumbing got to do with ghosts? Even if there *are* ghosts, you don't think for a minute *we* could bring them back, do you? We'll just gag it up. The kids will love it, and think of all the dough we'll make!"

Hank was coming around. "Well" — and he dragged the words — "it might be all right."

" 'Course it'll be all right!" said J.D., and he stepped over to a dry area near the cell where the scroll had been discovered. Here he dropped to his knees facing the light, his back to the cell doorway. "Come over here and I'll show you." Unrolling the parchment, he spread it across a large flagstone, thick with the slimy mold of two centuries, using a few rusty links of chain and a couple of rocks to hold it open.

Hank, hesitatingly and with much trepidation, shuffled over and stood uneasily beside his friend. Looking down, he viewed the scroll, chewed his thumbnail, and whined, "We might just be asking for it, J.D.!"

"Aw, don't be so scared!"

"Who's scared?" Hank demanded angrily.

"Well, all right, then, hang loose, will ya? All I'm going to do is copy the funny marks and say the crazy words to show you how we'll work it in the seance gag."

Hank inclined his head, dug a thumb into his ear as he nursed the insult, and watched dubiously as J.D. drew the symbols into the thick green slime of the flagstone with his finger. "You made that line crooked," he announced with a show of authority. "It's more straight."

"It don't have to be perfect. This is just to show how we'll do it," retorted J.D.

"Well, it oughta be done right!" Hank exclaimed, feeling now that he had evened the score.

"Aum . . . Aum . . . Aum," moaned J.D., reading from the scroll. "Mananan . . . verbum . . . fo . . . fohat . . . kali yug! Aum, Aum, Aum, Mananan verbum fohat . . . kali yug! Aum, Aum, Aum, Mananan verbum fohat Aum, Aum, Aum . . . Mananan . . . verbum fohat . . . kali yug!" He halted, turned, and looked up at Hank. "Then someone who's dead . . . like . . ." His brow wrinkled in thought until his eye caught the signature on the parchment. "Oh, come to us, Lady Aldetha Stowecroft, come to us!" he wailed. "Aum, Aum, Aum . . . Mananan verbum . . ."

"Cut it, J.D., cut it!" Hank gasped, his face a sickly gray. "Did you have to use that name?"

J.D. opened his eyes and looked up at Hank. "Why not? It's as good as any," he said. Then he looked straight ahead, again closed his eyes, and, as Hank watched in horror, once more began his incantations.

Slowly, as he mouthed the words, a hazy mass of whitish substance, like floating milk, began to materialize in the doorway of the cell, only a few paces behind the boys. It began to darken and curdle into a translucent, black, oily mass that writhed and squirmed itself into the hunched shape of a filthy old hag with long stringy hair hanging like dead snakes around her ugly face and shoulders. Her mouth was twisted into a fiendish grin as she leered at the boys. She wore a black shroud, rotten with mold, the lower part charred as if by fire. From her neck, suspended by a cord, was a wooden plaque upon which was scrawled the legend, "This be a witch. May God have mercy on her soul."

One bony hand held a long crooked staff; the other, with long, sharp fingernails, reached out toward the boys as she slithered, like her cat, even closer.

"Aummm, Aummmmm, Aummmmm . . . verbum," groaned J.D. He was having a ball.

The air grew icy cold, and in the shaft gusts of wind made moaning sounds. The iron door of one of the cells moved, and the hinges squealed.

"Okay, okay!" Hank said nervously, "I get the idea! You don't have to overdo it."

J.D. stopped his spiritualistic efforts and grinned at him. "How am I doing?"

Hank grabbed J.D.'s arm and pulled him to his feet. "Maybe you're doing too good. Come on! I stayed, like you asked me to, and I listened to all that stuff. Now let's get out of here. I've had it!"

J.D. picked up the scroll and rolled it up.

"You see, Hank," he grinned, "what did I tell you? There's nothing in this spook jazz."

From the sky directly above the air shaft came a rip of lightning and a tremendous crash of thunder, and both boys fell to their knees. "Wow!" J.D. gasped. "That struck close!"

Then, Hank's dog, Butch, who had tracked his master down into the dungeon, made his grinning, tongue-lolling, tail-wagging appearance. Butch spotted the cat, and with a yowl of indignation scrambled after the animal. The cat arrowed through the close space between the boys. Then came Butch, sliding over the pavement and sloughing into Hank's knees. Diablo made three sensational bounds toward the stairs, and was gone. Butch twisted around, paws skidding, nails clawing; he was barking furiously as he headed after the cat.

"Holy cow!" yelled J.D. and, with Hank at his heels, clattered up the stairs after Butch. Bursting into the taproom, they ran to the front door. Through the steady drizzle of the spring rain came far-off receding yelps and howls, like something out of *The Voice of Bugle Ann*.

J.D. looked up at the clearing sky. "It's almost stopped raining, Hank," he announced.

"That's good," replied Hank. "I want to get out of this dump. It gives me the creeps!"

"Well, do you want to do it?"

"Do what . . . get out of here? Sure! I just said so, didn't I?"

"I didn't mean *that!* I mean put on the seance."

Hank walked to the door and, with the toe of his shoe, thoughtfully rearranged a small pile of rubble. "You sure it will be just Halloween stuff, huh?"

"Sure!" J.D walked to the low windowsill and sat down. "Sure, just like Halloween." Then, looking at the ceiling, he asked tentatively, "You . . . you don't want to be the medium, do you?"

Hank looked at him sharply; a guy had to be careful what he said when J.D came up with stuff like this. "What does the medium do?"

"He's the one that talks real spookylike . . . brings back the ghosts and junk." He glanced quickly at Hank with concern. "Like I just did . . . only in the dark. You want to do that part?"

"In the dark!" Hank exploded "Are you kidding? I don't want any part of it!"

"You sure?" J.D. grinned slyly.

"Sure, I'm sure! You be the medium. . . ." He paused. "I'll take tickets."

"You don't take tickets at a seance!" J.D. rose disgustedly from his seat, walked to the center of the room, picked up a spike, examined it, then threw it out of the window. "I know what!" he exclaimed. "You can be the ghost!"

Hank stared at J.D. "Ghost! . . . what ghost?"

"Any old ghost! We can have it over in my cellar. We'll fix up a place so it will be real dark, see? And I'll shut my eyes, and" — he gestured with the scroll — "read this stuff here. Then you come in covered with a sheet, and say, 'Who's got my head?' or something. The kids will eat it up!"

A pleading look crossed Hank's features. "Can't I just take tickets, J.D.?"

J.D. was deep in thought; then his face came up with an inspired grin. "Hey! How's about using Blackbeard the Pirate for the ghost? You could dress up with a beard . . ."

Hank was horrified. "J.D., are you nuts?" He lowered his voice. "Blackbeard used to live right here in this house!"

"So who *cares?*" cried J.D. in agonized annoyance. Then, making a big show of his disgust, he turned his back on Hank and in a mocking voice said loudly, "It was indeed a pleasure visiting your palace, Mr. Blackbeard! I hope you like the new gas station you're getting." He gave Hank another look of disdain and moved resolutely toward the door. "It's stopped raining," he said.

Hank angrily kicked at some trash. "Ouch!" he yelped, and hurriedly limped after J.D. "But we could be sticking our necks out! Can't we use some guy that lived farther away? How about it, J.D.," he asked as he stepped out onto the porch, "do we *have* to use Blackbeard?"

# 2: SUNDAY

# 6

THE BOYS worked furiously all day Sunday setting up the equipment needed for the performance on Sunday afternoon. In the excitement of starting something new, even Hank had become inspired, and forgetting his fears, had thrown himself into the plan with enthusiasm.

Now all was in readiness. The news of the seance and the fact that ghosts were involved had spread like wildfire. There was an overwhelming demand for seats, but the boys decided it would be wiser to limit this first venture into the spirit world to a few of the more impressionable younger children. Shows for their contemporaries could be staged at a later date, and at increased rates.

J.D.'s costume was intended to be a sort of Hindu affair. As a matter of fact, it was the same costume he wore when he conducted his magic shows. He had no idea what kind of costume a medium wore, but this one seemed perfect for the role.

A man's brightly colored silk dressing gown was the most effective part of the outfit — a gift from Mr. Jones's mother-in-law two Christmases back, which Mr. Jones refused to wear. "Wear that thing?" he had exclaimed. "What if someone saw me!" And, of course, Mrs. Jones could scarcely give it away!

A bath towel wound around J.D.'s head made the perfect turban, especially when surmounted by a large pink ostrich plume he had discovered at the bottom of a trunk. Around his waist was an emerald-green sash, and a burnt-cork mustache and goatee completed the flamboyant ensemble. J.D. was quite pleased with himself.

He and Hank had partitioned off a small area of the cellar by hanging worn-out blankets and a tarpaulin from the overhead beam. This provided a dark and gloomy room, a perfect setting for a seance.

The curtains parted and Hank stepped out, dressed as Blackbeard. His costume was equally as impressive as J.D.'s. Somewhere the boys had found a gigantic black beard with curved wires that went over the ears. It was a remarkable imitation of the real thing, although it had the disturbing habit of slipping off when least expected. Hank wore a heavy black overcoat cut off at mid-thigh, as mangy-looking as the beard. His Boy Scout shorts and his father's old hat, the brim pinned up into a tricorn style, completed the picture. Around his waist he wore one of his sister's best belts, a wide leather affair with a big silver buckle. "Criminy," he told J.D., "if she ever knew I had this!" Into the belt was shoved a big plastic pistol.

"You look great!" J.D. grinned. He was looking at the draperies with satisfaction. He turned to Hank. "Where did you put the flour? Those kids will be here any minute."

"Can't we just skip that part?"

"Are you kidding?" J.D. parted the draperies and ducked inside with Hank at his heels. "C'mon, where did you put it?"

Hank expelled a long breath of resignation. Holding his beard in place, he reached under the round table which occupied the center of the area, and came up with a flour sifter, which he handed to J.D. A kerosene lantern hung from the ceiling, casting a dismal light over the enclosure. Around the table were arranged a few boxes and chairs.

J.D. cranked the flour sifter, spreading a film of flour over the table. In the light of the lantern it looked as yellow as sulphur. "Remember," he said officiously, "to come in when I say 'Aum . . . Aum . . . Aum.' " He paused, wrinkled his brow, pulled out the

scroll and studied it. "Mananan . . . verbum . . ."

He looked at Hank, who was again adjusting
the precarious hold of the beard on his bat-
wing ears. "And try and cut down on the noise
when you crawl in and move the table." He
studied the beard. "Why don't you get some
adhesive tape for those whiskers, so they'll stay
on?"

J.D. put the sifter on the floor and covered it
with the bottom of the drapery. "Now, don't
forget to snap on the flashlight! You got the
flashlight?"

"Sure, I've got the flashlight. It's in my
pocket."

The parchment looked even more yellow
and ancient in the depressing light. J.D.'s
lips moved silently as he rehearsed the magic
words.

Hank sank onto one of the chairs and
watched him apprehensively; old fears were
creeping back. "I still don't like this business,"
he said. "My dad was telling about a polter
. . . polter-something-or-other, that haunted
his grandmother's house."

J.D. looked up abruptly. "A *what*?"

"A . . . a . . . poltergeist."

"A poltergeist? What the heck is a poltergeist?"

"It's some kind of a ghost . . . the kind
that goes around pushing things over. Anyhow, this one did!"

J.D. observed his friend with mingled interest and disdain. He slowly rolled up the parchment and put it into his pocket. "You mean," he said, "it was a *real ghost?*" he sniffed. "You're kidding!"

"Oh yeah?" Hank exclaimed, as he removed his beard. "The heck I am! His grandma had this big bed, and on top of each of the four posts was a brass ball. When nobody slept there, every morning they'd find the balls on the pillow. But when anybody slept in the room, nothing happened!"

J.D. stared at him and snorted, "I don't believe it!"

Hank stood up. "Okay, go ask my dad! He'll tell you! All kinds of funny things happened in that house. Caught fire three times!"

"Yeah? Then what?"

"No one would buy it, so they tore it down."

"What kind of a ghost did your father say it was?"

"A poltergeist."

The Great Hindu Swami's hand moved slowly to his pocket and withdrew the scroll. He was examining it with newborn concern when there came a pounding on the cellar door, and shrill cries of "J.D. . . . Hank . . ." His concentration was interrupted, and the opportunity lost forever to question the advisability of going on with the seance. Poltergeists were forgotten. He shoved the scroll back into his pocket and whispered loudly, "Get out of sight, Hank! I'll let them in!"

Hank scurried around behind the draperies, hooking the wires of the beard over his ears, while J.D. marched regally toward the cellar door and swung it wide. Two boys and four girls, all younger than J.D., poured, jabbering and squealing, into the basement and crowded around him.

"You gonna tell ghost stories, J.D.?"

"Hey! Where's Hank?"

The youngest, Judy, going-on-six with big blue eyes, proclaimed, "My mommy said you better not scare me!" She clung fearfully to the hand of an older girl named Joyce.

J.D. eyed Joyce with considerable distaste. "Holy cow, Joyce," he grumbled, "what did you have to bring *her* along for?"

"I had to," said Joyce. "I'm baby-sitting."

"Well, if she starts bawling, you take her right home! This isn't kid stuff!" He turned away and walked toward the draped area. The group, chattering noisily, flocked after him. At the sight of the dismal drapes, all of them were crestfallen; they had expected something far more spectacular than this! They wailed their disapproval.

"Aw, J.D., ain't you gonna have a stage?"

"Yeah! What happened to the stage you had fixed up? Don't you need a stage like you had for the magic shows?"

"Yeah, J.D., what's all that junk hanging there for, J.D.?"

J.D. didn't say a word. He held the draperies aside and the babbling ceased. As they filed inside, their voices became hushed whispers, *ooh's* and *aah's,* and small giggles.

J.D. carefully closed the draperies behind him and, when he spoke, his voice had the funereal tones of a pompous undertaker. "Take your places around the table, please!" He bowed, went to a high-backed, carved chair, vintage Sears Roebuck 1920, and sat rigidly. He closed his eyes, as if in deep thought.

It was like being in a tent, a square tent whose high walls were a hodgepodge of loosely hung, faded blankets and stained, dirty canvas. As the children sat around the table, the area behind and beneath them was solid with shadow, like a bowl half filled with black ink, and the walls soaked it up like a blotter. In a weak yellow light the tabletop seemed to be floating and bobbing in gloomy space.

"Isn't it spooky, Joyce?" said one of the girls.

An older boy, one whom J.D. and Hank usually referred to as "that wise guy," began to intone, "Mary, I'm on the first step! Mary, I'm on . . ."

Amid shrieks of laughter, J.D. leaped to his feet. "Okay, you kids! Shut up if you want to see the seance! I won't do it if anybody does any more talking!" He glared venomously at the group seated around the table, "I mean it, now!" he warned.

"What's this yellow stuff?" asked Judy innocently, and her hand darted forward and smeared through the flour. J.D. howled, "Don't touch that! It's magic dust!"

Judy jerked her hand away, and her eyes widened as she stared apprehensively at the yellow dust on her palm. There was a moment of concentrated silence as six heads bent over the strange powder. J.D. found the sifter and repaired the damage.

"What *is* that stuff?" one of the boys repeated.

J.D. put the sifter away. "I told you, it's magic dust!" he growled, "and cut the talking!" He waited until there was absolute silence, then he cleared his throat, closed his eyes, and announced that he was about to go into a trance and bring back the ghost of Blackbeard the Pirate. "O Blackbeard," he wailed, "can you hear me . . . ?"

"Where's Hank?" asked Judy. "Isn't he going to be in it, too? He said he was."

The medium's eyes blinked. He glowered at Judy, who continued to look at him with innocent and wondering eyes. "Shhh!" said the older girl. "Hank will be in it; just wait."

J.D. closed again his eyes. "O Blackbeard," he moaned, "can you hear me calling you?" He stretched his arms upward. His face twisted as if he were suffering unendurable agony, and he groaned and wailed amid half-smothered giggles from his audience. "Captain Edward Teach . . . hear me! I, the great Swami, call to you. Black . . . beard!" The giggles became shrieks of laughter."

The Swami was angry. "Okay, you kids, cut the comedy, or I'll quit right now."

"Aw, c'mon, J.D.," said Joyce. "We'll be quiet."

"I want to go home," whined Judy.

"You all promise?" The response was encouraging, and J.D. rose to his feet. "Oh, come to us, spirit of Captain Teach! Oh, come to us, ghost of Blackbeard, the greatest pirate that ever lived!"

He paused, and with eyes closed, acted as though he were listening. Then he said, "Yes, master, I shall obey. I shall draw the magic lines of Satan in the magic dust."

J.D. opened his eyes and, with his finger, traced the cabalistic symbols in the flour.

For the first time, he attracted an eager and attentive audience. "Aum . . . Aum . . . Aum . . . !" he called loudly, and saw the draperies opposite him move slightly. "Mananan verbum fohat . . ." The table began to rock, and the children screamed with delight, not one of them aware of Hank's lanky figure snaking slowly upward from the inky blackness behind them.

"O kali yug . . . Aum . . . Aum . . . Aum," J.D. groaned. "Are you with us? Are you with us, O Captain Teach? Yes, yes . . . now I feel your presence!"

Concealed within the voluminous folds of his coat, Hank had the flashlight ready to shine upward on his face. He snapped it on just as the beard slipped. J.D. waited until things were under control, then raised his arm stiffly and pointed a rigid finger at Hank. The imitation specter's eyes were wide with horror!

"Welcome, Blackbeard! Welcome!" said J.D. All eyes followed in the direction of the pointed finger, and there were cries of surprise and pleasure. Judy screamed, "Mama! *Mama!*"

The flashlight fell clattering to the concrete floor, rolled, and clicked against a chair leg. The beard came loose, but Hank ignored it. His face had turned a sickly green. He stood rigidly, eyes goggling at something behind J.D. In the air was the acrid smell of burning gunpowder. Hank pointed a shaking lip at the area above J.D.'s head and from his lips came a hoarse whisper: "B-b-behind you, J.D.!"

There was no laughter now, only puzzled frowns. J.D. was annoyed and mystified. Leave it to Hank to louse things up! He turned back to his friend, whose palsied arm was still outstretched. Hank's eyes were closed, and he swayed like a pine tree ready to topple. "What's up, Hank? Is this a gag?" J.D. rasped.

But Hank was out on his feet. Stiff as a ramrod, his shoulders went back against the draperies and, slowly and majestically, he slid to the floor.

"I wanna go home!" Judy howled.

J.D. scrambled from his seat and knelt beside his friend. "Holy cow! Hank fainted!"

He stared from Hank to the space behind the Sears Roebuck chair, then whirled toward the children. "I don't see anything. . . . Do you see anything?" They gaped at him and shook their heads. Judy started to cry and buried her head in Joyce's lap.

Behind the chair loomed the ghost of Captain Edward "Blackbeard" Teach. His features were wreathed in smoke from the fuses in his beard, and wet strands of seaweed hung from his shoulders. As J.D. turned back to Hank, this monster grinned and winked!

# 7

IT WAS THAT MAGIC HOUR just after sun-
down. The bright spring sky had faded into
hazy tints of topaz; the street lamps glowed
like overambitious fireflies, casting light nowhere. The tall trees encircling Godolphin's
old courthouse were green-black shadows, and
the statue of Robert Maynard, with the cowering pirates at his feet, was an ugly silhouette.

From Pamlico Sound came the hoot of a
tramp steamer, slogging its way toward Ocracoke Inlet and the sea. The delicious smell of
freshly popped corn, issuing from a portable
stand parked at the curb, had made eager customers of J.D. and Hank. Mechanically the
vender filled their order.

"Put a lot of butter on it," commanded J.D.
Each boy put his share of the cost upon the

counter. They had discovered you didn't get as much if you bought two fifteen-cent boxes, so it was one very large package the vender handed to Hank. Carrying the box, the boys drifted off to a park bench some distance away and sat down. Hank held the box in front of J.D., who dug deep, getting a large handful.

"I wasn't kidding, J.D.! You looked *right at him!* He was standing right behind you, big as life! Don't tell me I was seeing things!" He chewed vigorously. "I warned you it might work."

J.D. nonchalantly flipped some corn into his mouth. "None of the other kids saw him. You just thought you saw something." He reached for more — but a big, dirty, hairy hand beat him to it. The monstrous paw projected from a cuff decorated with a row of brass buttons.

Astounded, the boys stared at the digging hand, followed it with their eyes as it withdrew and carried the popcorn to the bearded face. Captain Edward Teach, ex-skipper of the *Queen Anne's Revenge,* leaned back on the bench and lazily tossed the popcorn into his mouth. His enormous beard was bedecked with a multitude of tiny ribbons and the remains of burned-out cannon fuses. Two long braids of coal-black hair hung from his ears to his shoulders, while the rest was a tangle of oily filth. A few strands of seaweed still clung to his coat.

Incongruously, his tricorn hat bore aloft
J.D.'s pink ostrich plume pinned to its side.
He chewed noisily and with gusto, and his
belch resounded as loudly as the recent hoot of
the steamer. He pushed his hat back on his
head and reached for more popcorn. Hank
held the box in a paralyzed clutch, or he would
surely have dropped it.

The pirate jiggled the popcorn in his hand,
studied it carefully before popping it into his
mouth, chewed, swallowed, made sucking
noises through his back teeth, and picked at
them with a thumbnail. Without removing his
thumb, he announced with authority, "Ain't
near as good as what the Injuns make," and
brushed the crumbs from his beard and his
coat. This article of attire was the only clean
and neat thing about him, and it blazed with
rows of brass buttons. With it he wore greasy
pantaloons, and his legs were encased in large
boots.

A policeman passing on his beat smiled at
the boys. "Hi," he said pleasantly, "nice evening, isn't it?" and continued up the street.
Hank sat rigid, staring straight ahead. J.D.
gawked after the policeman in astonishment.
Holy cow! he thought wildly. He can't *see*
him! He looked at Hank, whose only move-
ment was his Adam's apple, rising and falling
with every gulp.

"Yup," said Teach, "parched maize be the
stuff to raise a swab's thirst, I always say." He

grinned at the boys. "Yessiree, lads, a mighty thirst!" and he reached for more popcorn.

After another interval of chewing and belching, the terror of land and sea drew a long knife from his belt and picked his teeth with the point of the blade. Leaning over toward Hank, he nudged him in the ribs with the handle, winked, and growled, "D'ye happen to know lad, where an old sea dog might get himself a spot o' rum? Ol' Teach ain't had s'much as a drop since I run into that scrovie Bob Maynard over yonder." He gestured with a thumb over his shoulder at the statue.

"Back in 1718, it were. Like to have cut his gullet out and et it, too, I did. But the lobster snuck up behind me and done me in, he did." He helped himself to more popcorn. "Ye looks to ol' Teach like a couple o' bright lads . . . and Godolphin Town being all growed the way it has has got Teach a mite off course. Lost his bearings, he has. Now, speak up, me lads! Where can a body git a spot o' rum?"

He leaned forward, placing his elbows upon his knees and, turning his massive head, looked J.D. squarely in the face. His brutish features were gradually transformed by a broad smile. "What be the matter, mateys, the cat got your tongues?"

The beaming smile thawed some of J.D.'s fears, and he almost forgot that he was being addressed by a ghost. "Y-y-y-you can't buy rum here . . . sir! This here is a dry county."

Teach snapped his torso upright, his cutlass clashed against the bench, and Hank spilled the popcorn. "Dry county?" he roared. "Bash me binnacle! What be a dry county?" His scowling gaze swept up and down the street and the park behind him. Then he reached inside his jacket and scratched his ribs. "Ye mean just because it don't rain fer a spell, a body can't buy rum?"

"Oh, no, sir!" J.D. replied. "I mean it's against the law to sell liquor in Godolphin County."

Teach slowly settled back on the bench, moved his hat back an inch, and contemplatively scratched his chin beneath his beard. "Now effen that ain't the scroviest kettle o' fish! A swab be'n't able to buy himself a spot o' rum in Godolphin Town." For a long moment he was deep in thought. Suddenly, he leaped to his feet and angrily paced back and forth in front of the cringing boys, scratching his back and growling like a bear.

Abruptly, he stopped and snapped his fingers. "Mark'ee, lads! I lay a tuppence that seagoing rum skutch Bob Maynard had his scurvy hand in this! Swoggle me eyes effen ol' Teach ain't gallied! Maynard be always trying to sink good honest seamen, he were, and getting right fine wages for it too!" He continued his thoughtful pacing, but finally his face brightened. "Hang me from Tyburn Tree, mateys, but rain or no rain, honest ol' Teach knows where there be rum!"

His little pig eyes darted from side to side, and he pushed his face close to the boys'. Breath reeking of garlic, he croaked secretively out of one side of his mouth, "Me Boar's Head's where it will be!" He stood erect and grinned, and J.D. and Hank stared at each other. "Now," he rumbled, "fetch more o' the maize, lads." Neither of them stirred. "Lively now, I say! Where be the scurvy lobscouser what has got the parched maize?"

He studied them as if he were examining two strange dead fish, then he burst into roars of laughter. "Well, shiver me timbers! Aye, it be'n't the first time ol' Blackbeard scared a body stiff! Never ye minds, lads, I'll find the belly-robbing sea cook what has ye maize, meself!"

With that, he sniffed the air, and grinning, hitched up his pants and headed with a rolling gait toward the source of the popcorn smell. For an instant both boys hesitated. Then both scrambled to their feet and dashed across the lawn toward the statue of Robert Maynard, throwing themselves flat against the ground behind it. For several moments they lay gasping, not daring to move. "We can't stay here forever!" J.D. whispered.

Together they slowly rose and peered between the sturdy legs of Blackbeard's worst enemy, back at the bench where they had sat.

J.D.'s face was tense. "Can you see him, Hank?" he whispered. "I can't. Where do you suppose he went?"

Hank's eyes were round green grapes. "No, he's gone! Right in front of my eyes he faded out!"

Within the popcorn wagon, the vender was whistling the latest popular tune as he filled a box. He expected a rush of business in about a half hour. Suddenly, the box of popcorn was snatched from his hand — vanished! — and his whistle died like a tire going flat.

Meanwhile, J.D. and Hank had crept stealthily from behind the base of the statue, and were cautiously skirting a clump of bushes when they were petrified by the sound of Teach's voice, not ten feet away. "Ho, me lads," he roared. As one, they dived into the bushes. Teach eyed the moving branches and chuckled. "Have a bit o' parched maize, lads!"

Under the spreading branches, J.D. and Hank sank their bodies into the turf and went rigid.

"Holy cow!" J.D. breathed.

Between the low-hanging branches, they watched the pirate's booted foot go up on tiptoe and steal toward where they lay shaking in terror. Hank's fingers dug into J.D.'s arm. The boots came to a halt, spread far apart, then began rocking from heel to toe, just three feet from their heads.

At that terrifying instant, from up the street came the rapid click of high heels on hard pavement, and the boots turned in the direction of the sound. J.D. couldn't see the pirate's sly, mischievous grin turn into a sickly-sweet

smile. As for Hank, he couldn't see it, either;
his head was buried under his arms.

The girl approaching was about as pretty a
lass as any Blackbeard had ever seen, and he
whipped off his hat. As she tripped by, his
huge figure jackknifed into an elegant bow.
Unfortunately, the tribute went unseen, and
the girl clicked on up the street.

Teach indignantly stared after her. Didn't
she know who he was? Didn't he have the
reputation of being the boldest pirate on land
or sea, especially where the fair sex was
concerned? Just because he was a ghost didn't
mean he was going to change! The frown
quickly became a grin, and giving his belt a
hitch, he followed her with his usual rolling
gait.

He pursued the girl to the corner of Main
Street and Second Avenue, where he deject-
edly watched her run into the arms of a weak-
looking young man wearing horn-rimmed
glasses. This individual, it seemed to Teach,
was more interested in something tied to his
wrist than he was in the pretty lass. He kept
pointing at it and grumbling about how late
she was. With a snort of disgust, the pirate
turned from the pair and made his way up
Main Street.

The busy avenue was alive with strollers
enjoying the balmy evening, and Teach became his old gay self again. He chuckled. "The
old town be having a heap more pretty wenches
than it usta," he thought, as he rambled along

the broad sidewalk, stuffing popcorn into his mouth and bowing low to each girl that passed. But mark'ee! They be catching the ague for sure, running afore the wind in nothing but a shift!

The boys followed him, but at a considerable distance, now and then ducking into a convenient doorway, and watching with alarm the progress of this fantastic ghost that only they could see.

They saw him sneak up behind a dignified man and flip his Homburg hat over his eyes. They watched the man whirl around with a grunt of indignation, and heard Blackbeard's roar of laughter at his victim's puzzled consternation.

The neon signs particularly caught his fancy, the way they blinked and buzzed and were so bright. He squeezed a glowing tube between his fingers, as he so often had snuffed out a candle. The glass crunched, and the entire sign went dark. Blackbeard gasped, his jaw hanging in amazement. "Jakers!" He grinned slyly up at another and tossed away the empty popcorn box. It was a much larger sign than the first, and he found it necessary to climb an adjacent telephone pole to reach it. He gave the blazing red tube a quick squeeze.

After that, one by one, every glowing and urgent demand for attention on Main Street went out of business. Outraged shopkeepers stormed, but most of their potential customers remarked on how much nicer the street looked without those awful signs!

Having finished with this exhilarating sport, and the unintentional bit of civic improvement, the pirate started to cross the busy thoroughfare in the middle of the block. This, of course, was even more dangerous for Blackbeard's type of ghost than it was for a living person because, although J.D. and Hank could see him, no one else could, and unlike an ordinary ghost, he was solid — real solid. You couldn't shove your hand through him. He was a poltergeist and had invisible substance. Therefore, Blackbeard had to be careful, especially about cars. But cars were something he had a lot to learn about.

Blithely, he stepped down off the curb, and within a second, was roaring and skipping about like a wounded banshee, dodging cars that whizzed by him faster than anything he ever dreamed of. Somehow, and very luckily, he reached the comparative safety of the middle of the street, losing most of his pride and dignity somewhere on the way. With cutlass drawn he glared at the insolent speeding demons swooshing by. For an hour he had wandered the streets in search of his old home, and the more he looked the more confused he became.

Suddenly the headlights of a car pulling out of a driveway flooded the Boar's Head with light. The moving glare marched vertical tree-trunk shadows across the gray façade. Teach saw it and screeched with joy. Motorists, mistaking the screech for a police siren, skidded their cars to a halt. For a long moment Blackbeard stared at his pride and joy, then, as if in a daze, stepped from the curb to the street and followed a zig-zag course between the waiting cars toward the old structure. His eyes were shining as he moved faster and faster, and his cutlass slapped against his thigh as he stomped and clanked up to the gate.

He didn't open the gate, but leaned on the fence, arms wide-stretched, the point of a picket clutched in each hand. Abruptly his grin collapsed and his face darkened into a scowl. A large sign had caught his eye. It was new, and the fresh paint gleamed. Gigantic crisp, black-and-red letters stated that on this location soon a new Summit Oil Company gasoline station would be erected, and below was a picture of the station-to-be. It was wildly "modern," consisting of an arrangement of sharp straight lines combined with juts and angles that zoomed, curved, and whistled off in every direction — lines and forms that fulfilled no function except to attract attention. It was as if the building had been frozen in the process of blowing up. On the very bottom of the sign, prominently displayed, was "J.R. Maynard Construction Company."

Blackbeard yanked open the gate and, as he passed through, his heels crunched and dug into the gravel path. He stopped in front of the sign. Completely bewildered, he shook his head and turned his attention to the Boar's Head. Now his eyes filled with sadness and dismay; they grew moist and he blinked. Pulling a colorful rag from the side pocket of his coat, he noisily blew his nose.

"Did you hear that?" asked a voice from the street behind him. "Place is haunted, that's for sure!"

Teach turned his head. An elderly couple were standing on the sidewalk looking at the Boar's Head. "Glad they're going to tear that eyesore down," continued the man.

"Why, Albert, it's a shame," cried the woman, "that's what it is! It ought to be restored! It could be such a pretty place, if it was just fixed up a bit. Betty Rheberger was saying the other day that it used to belong to a pirate."

"Yep," said the man, "I heard that story too. Don't put much stock in it, but old sourpuss Maynard sure got a pretty penny for the place. Been in his family for years."

"I still think it's a pity," she insisted, "to tear down such a historic relic, and all those beautiful trees, too, just to build an ugly gas station. Someone ought to stop them!"

Blackbeard's face was a thundercloud. He shot a look at the sign, the Boar's Head, then back at the couple. They had started on up the street. With one hand Teach lifted the brim of his hat, and scratching his head, watched the figures until they were out of sight.

By day the taproom of the tavern was a

dreary place; by night it was ten times worse.
The moving headlights of passing cars sten-
ciled weird moving shapes on the peeling
plaster walls, creating a veritable convention
hall of banshees, ghosts, goblins, and just plain
spooks. Street noises were remote, adding to
the eerie aspect.

Blackbeard entered the taproom, his bulk
making the ceiling seem even lower. Grinning
his delight, he looked about with a familiar
eye, but as he took in the tattered hanging
wallpaper, the piles of debris and dust on the
floor, and the cluttered stacks of splintered
lumber, his face clouded. "Ain't the way Aldetha usta keep the place!" he grumbled. Over
a windowsill peered the wide eyes of J.D. and
Hank. They watched the ghost stride to the
bar and pound on it with the palm of his
hand. "Ho, John!" he bellowed. "Ho, John
Clark, ye scrovie ol' sea wonk!" Courage
drained from the boys like the yolk from a
broken egg. Teach heard the scramble of their
feet as they dashed from the porch, and he
chuckled as he went to the door and watched
them skid around the fence post into Main
Street.

Still chuckling, he returned to the bar. "Ho,
Johnny!" he roared again in his deep, rumbling voice. " 'Tis Cap'n Ed'ard Teach aboard,
'tis, and mighty in need o' a nip o' Cape
Horn rainwater. Been in dry dock too long, he
has!"

Cocking his massive head to one side, he

listened expectantly, but his only answer was the distant blast of a ship's whistle and the raucous tooting of a traffic jam. Lights from the street danced an Indian war dance over his face and figure and on the wall behind him.

In the long, dismal hallway he frowned, squinted, and with his knuckles, vigorously rubbed his nose. Then, giving his belt a hitch, he ambled toward the room at the far end, the floor boards creaking and complaining under his weight. "Hit war somewhere in here," he muttered, and nosed about the room, shoving rubbish and plaster rubble right and left with his booted foot. "Ah, hah!" he chortled. "This be it!" Dropping to his knees, he drew his cutlass and with the point pried up the corner of a plank, the rusty nails protesting as the board came loose. This he tossed aside, and reached down an arm's length into the opening, his cheek flat against the floor. His worried look became a grin of triumph when his searching hand found and clutched an old dusty bottle.

The Captain sat in the middle of a patch of moonlight and yanked the cork. He hoisted the bottle high above his face and grinned at it. "Here's to ye, Bob Maynard," he boomed, "ye orphin-cheating ol' sea toad! Here's to ye and your scrovie ol' dry-weather drinking laws!"

## 8

J. D. AND HANK scuffed down Main Street
toward the waterfront and the small park that
was called Maynard Square, putting distance
between themselves and the Boar's Head Tavern. They had discussed every angle of the
position they were in, the ghastly phenomenon
they had created, as well as possible ways of
getting out of the mess. They had come up
with nothing. There was no way out!

Both were very much aware of how potent
this monster could be, and J.D. remembered
how cold and solid Blackbeard's sheathed cutlass had felt earlier that evening, when it accidentally banged against his leg. Why, this
ghost could actually kill someone! He men-

tioned this to Hank, and added, "It's like being Frankenstein and creating a monster." Hank scoffed, "Yah . . . but that was only a movie; this is for real!"

In the park they carefully avoided the bench upon which they had first met their ghostly pirate friend and chose one close by the popcorn wagon. The street light above spread a comforting light, and the boys felt comparatively safe. They slouched on the bench, feet sprawled out before them, hands stuffed deep in trouser pockets. For a long time they sat in depressed silence; then Hank said, "Feel like some popcorn, J.D.?"

J.D. moodily eyed the wagon. "Naw," he grumbled, "I ain't hungry."

"I guess I ain't hungry, neither."

"D'you suppose he's gone?"

"Who?"

"*Who!*" J.D. blurted. "Who d'you suppose?"

"Oh! . . . Yeah! . . . Golly, I hope so!"

Again there was silence. Suddenly J.D. grabbed Hank's arm. "Hey! Did you see that cover move?"

"Huh?"

"That sewer cover, the one near the curb . . . by the wagon. Did you see it move?"

Hank squinted from J.D. to the cover his friend was pointing at. "Uh uh, I didn't see it . . . *Hey!* . . . *Jeepers* . . . It *did* move!"

Both scrambled bolt upright. J.D.'s knuckles whitened as his fingers dug into Hank's arm.

The cover was jiggling up and down, making hollow sounds. Then it erupted and soared, landing flat on the pavement ten feet away. There it wobbled and clattered like a gigantic silver dollar.

The popcorn vender scrambled out of his wagon. J.D. and Hank lingered only long enough to watch a hairy hand clutching a bottle come up out of the sewer and place the precious article on the pavement beside the opening. By the time another hand appeared, followed by a bearded face, the boys were on their way.

"It must've been some kind of gas explosion in the sewer system," the vender explained to any in the small crowd who would listen.

No one saw the real cause, or heard him grunt as he climbed out of the sewer. Teach picked up his bottle, hiccupped, and eyed the manhole. "Folks got escape hatches all over town," he muttered. "Wonder who be the rum skutches they be trying to get away from." Noticing the group gathered on the sidewalk, Teach grinned and performed a lavish bow. "A bow like this'n," he exulted as he swept the street with his hat, "would make that scurvy Eden greener as seaweed."

As he lurched and rolled up Main Street, these bows became more frequent. He was singing in a deep bass voice, holding the neck of the bottle in one hand and waving his cutlass like a baton in the other.

"Oh, blow, ye winds, yo ho,
Oh, blow, ye winds, yo ho,
The *Queen Anne's Revenge* is a tidy ship
So blow, ye winds, yo ho!"

Chanting lustily, he passed within a few feet
of the boys, cowering between two parked cars.

"I still can't figure out," whispered J.D. after
he had passed, "why nobody can see or hear
him 'cept *us!*"

"Yeah," replied Hank, his eyes following the
boisterous pirate up the street. "But like I told
you, you never should have fooled around
with that magic stuff. You're the kook that said
there was no such thing as a ghost! Not only
that, look at the condition he's in!"

J.D. knew that it was really his fault, and
the mantle of responsibility settled about his
soul like a shroud. He remembered the words
of the magic scroll, especially the incomplete
sentence that read, "Let these words o' black
magic bring misery to . . ." As he peered up
the street at the ghost, the shroud became icy
cold.

Night and the arching branches of the trees
had transformed Elm Street into a quiet, deserted green tunnel, lined with houses and
gleaming windows that revealed people moving aimlessly about, watching TV, or reading
newspapers. Bugs and moths flitted, smacked,
and batted into street lamps. A lawn sprinkler
lazily revolved.

Within this tunnel, J.D. and Hank came to

halt in front of the Jones residence. "Well
. . . see you in the morning, Hank."

"Yeah, see you," replied the tall boy. He
started to go, hesitated, and scanned the street
in every direction. "I sure hope," he said, "that
. . . you-know-who doesn't show up again!"

"Yeah, me too!"

Halfway up his porch steps, J.D. stopped
and called after Hank, whose long legs were
rapidly scissoring him toward his home next
door. He was going to ask if it would be all
right if he stayed overnight at Hank's house.
"Yeah?" Hank answered from his own porch.

"Oh . . . nothing," said J.D., changing his
mind. "It wasn't important," and he jogged up
the rest of the steps. Two screen doors banged
in rapid succession.

In the shadows, Blackbeard leaned his invisible shoulder against the trunk of a tree,
crossed his legs, picked at a back tooth with a
thumbnail, and chuckled.

J.D. entered the living room. Mr. Jones was
stretched out with his stocking feet on the
chintz-covered sofa near the fireplace. From
behind his newspaper, blue clouds of smoke
rose and lazily curled about the lamp above
his head. Mrs. Jones was knitting, and one
completed sleeve hung from her lap to the
floor. Above her, on the mantel of the fireplace,
stood the large, ornate porcelain vase which
was her pride and joy. She looked up. "Oh,
J.D. You startled me . . . I didn't hear you
come in!"

Mr. Jones lowered the newspaper to his lap, removed his pipe from his mouth, and said, "Kind of late to be prowling the streets, isn't it, son?"

"Aw, Dad, it ain't late!"

"Isn't," prompted Mrs. Jones.

Mr. Jones glanced at the monstrous grandfather's clock that stood in the corner. "Late enough . . . there's school tomorrow." He went back to his paper.

"Where were you all evening?" Mrs. Jones asked.

J.D. shot a frightened glance into the darkened entrance hallway. He thought he had heard the front door open. He came around slowly. "Huh?" he said.

Mrs. Jones laid down her knitting and studied her son. "I asked you where you were all evening."

"I was with Hank . . . we were in the park . . . different places."

The only illumination was provided by the two lamps his parents were using, and for the first time, J.D. realized how gloomy the room could be. He shuffled about peering into dark corners, then snapped on a wall switch, flooding the room with light.

"Turn those lights off, J.D.!" commanded his mother. "We have enough light. If you knew what our light bill is every month!" She looked at him closely. "You look pale. Are you feeling sick?"

J.D. snapped off the lights. "Aw, Mom! I feel all right!"

"Well, stop fidgeting! Have you got all of your homework done?"

"Uh huh."

"Well, get a book and read."

On the desk was a book he had started. Now he went there, sat, but could not bring himself to read. He strained his eyes, trying to penetrate the gloomy shadows. He remembered how, in the park, the ghost had mysteriously vanished, then just as quickly reappeared, and he was almost positive he had heard the front door open.

"Mom, can I turn on the TV?"

"No," said his mother without looking up, "you look at TV too much as it is. Anyway, it disturbs your father."

J.D. groaned, turned to his book, and tried to concentrate. He picked up a pencil and chewed it. The grandfather's clock clunked off the seconds like a trip hammer.

"Dad . . ."

"Hmmnnn?" said his father, and a cloud of smoke appeared above his newspaper.

"Dad, did you ever hear of a poltergeist?"

"A what?"

"A poltergeist."

The newspaper came down. "A *poltergeist?*"

Mrs. Jones, without stopping her knitting, interrupted. "Certainly, John," she smiled, "you know what a poltergeist is. Don't you remember Sam Oberteuffer telling about the one in his grandmother's house? It's a ghost, a very *stupid* kind of ghost, that goes around causing mischief. I think he said this one kept pushing knobs or something off a bed."

"Brass balls," put in J.D. "Four of them."

Mr. Jones rapped the ashes from his pipe. "You don't believe all that rubbish, I hope!" He put the stem of his dead pipe back between his teeth, and disappeared behind the paper.

"I don't know, John. Sam was pretty positive. If it is true, I should think it would be rather annoying to have such a horrible creature around."

"It's a lot of imagination, Alice, so forget it!"

"But, Dad," J.D. insisted, "there *could* be . . . huh?"

The pages of the newspaper crackled as Mr. Jones turned them. "Quit talking nonsense, J.D., and read your book."

"But holy cow, Dad, I seen . . ." J.D.'s wide eyes were fixed upon his mother's ornate vase. Under its own power, the vase was inching along the mantelpiece toward certain destruction!

"Yeah," said Mr. Jones absently, his eyes glued to the paper, "what did you see?"

For a long moment, J.D. was transfixed with terror. He glanced at his parents. They were totally unaware of the impending disaster.

"Huh?" said Mr. Jones.

"Oh . . . nothing," J.D. mumbled, as he

cautiously rose from his seat and edged for the
fireplace. The vase was teetering on the brink;
as it went over, J.D. caught it like a football
The urn went crazy in his arms; it jerked
about trying to escape.

Mrs. Jones looked up in alarm. Words
choked from her throat. *"J.D.! Put that vase
down!* What in the world is the matter with
you?"

Instantly, the ceramic acrobatics quit, and
the urn once more behaved like an honest
Sheboygan work of art.

"Put it back!" she ordered. "Put it right
back before you break it! Why, I can't understand what ever got into you!"

J.D. gingerly placed it on the ledge, cautiously withdrawing his hands, but ready to
grab it the instant it moved. "It . . . it was
so close to the edge, Mom . . . I, I . . ." He
backed away, still keeping an eye on the precious base.

Mrs. Jones tightened her lips, shook her
head, and picked up her knitting. "It was perfectly all right where it was," she said. "And,
J.D., I appreciate your consideration . . . but
good heavens, did you have to bounce it around
like that? Why, you frightened me so!"

J.D. hung his head and flopped down into
his chair at the desk. He gave the rug a dis-
gusted scuff with his foot, and turned a pleading look toward his mother. "Mom, if you
only . . ." He looked fearfully around the
room, then back at his mother. "Mom, this

ghost business, I, I . . ." He looked at the
sweater, his body stiffened, and he clutched
the arms of the old swivel chair so tightly his
fingers ached. On the verge of panic, he silently breathed, "Oh, no!"

The sleeve of the sweater, started at the
cuff, was slowly unraveling! The thread of
yarn stretched taut across the floor, around
the base of the desk, then across the room,
disappearing around the corner into the dark
recesses of the hall. On and on went the diabolical destruction; one fourth of the sleeve
was already gone! From the hallway came a
low snicker.

Mrs. Jones glanced up at her husband. "Did
you hear a noise, John?"

"Uh-huh."

"I swear, thought I heard someone chuckle.
Did you hear anything, J.D.?"

J.D.'s foot was blindly trying to find and pin
down the thread of yarn, and at the same time
he was making a great show of concentration
on his book. Actually, this activity had been
so completely absorbing that he hadn't heard
the snicker. "Huh?" he grunted.

"I asked," repeated Mrs. Jones, "whether
you heard a sound like a chuckle?"

"No'm."

Mrs. Jones said, "Hmn," and went back
to her knitting, and J.D.'s foot found the cord.
He felt it jerk angrily as he pinned it to the
floor. His posture, however, was both ludi-

crous and uncomfortable, and when he spoke his voice was plaintive and high-pitched.

"Dad."

"Now what?"

"I'm sure there must be such a thing as a ghost! Today I . . ."

The newspaper crunched down onto his father's lap and, over his glasses, Mr. Jones impatiently glared at his son. "I tell you, all this stuff about ghosts is nonsense! All I've been getting around here lately is talk about ghosts. Let's drop it, huh?"

At that moment, the jerking string of yarn escaped and the unraveling resumed at an even more rapid pace. J.D. heard a deep chuckle of glee from the hall. He glanced at his parents, almost hoping they heard it, too, but apparently they hadn't, because Mrs. Jones merely put her knitting down and looked calmly at her husband. "Now, John," she said thoughtfully, "I wouldn't be too sure. There have been dozens of stories about that old house that Maynard owns. Blackbeard the Pirate used to live there."

Dad laughed. "Okay, have it your way. But if Blackbeard's ghost is hanging out in that old shack, he'd better do some house-hunting instead of house-haunting! They're going to tear that mess down."

Mrs. Jones picked up her knitting. "Yes, I know, and it's a pity. It should be preserved."

The unraveling hesitated.

"Why, I think," she continued, "that house is really a lovely place; all it needs is a coat of paint. And to think" — she paused in her knitting and dreamily added, "that Blackbeard, the most daring and exciting pirate who ever lived, was supposed to have built that house!"

The destruction of the sleeve came to an abrupt halt. The astonished boy watched the process reverse itself. The sleeve, as if by magic, was being reknit, and in a twinkling was once more whole!

"Blackbeard, daring? Hah!" scoffed Mr. Jones. "Why, he was nothing but an old fake . . . a bag of wind! Used to fix up his whiskers with fuses or something; then he'd light them to make himself look fierce and try and scare people. Joe Maynard told me all about him."

J.D. stared at his father in alarm, then sped a glance toward the hall.

"But, Dad," he whined expecting any second to see his father go up in a cloud of smoke, "Dad . . ."

Mr. Jones ignored him, turned his attention back to the paper, and added, "If that old fake is haunting any place, there's nothing to worry about."

*Wham!* The newspaper in his father's hands was batted to the ceiling and the loose pages floated down around the startled head of Mr. Jones. Dazed, he slowly sat up and gaped in wonder at the torn pieces remaining in his hands.

# 9

"I TELL YOU, SAM," cried Mr. Jones into the telephone, "it was the darndest thing!"

" 'Night, Dad," said J.D., as he edged by on his way up to his room.

Dad nodded and moved to one side. "Yeah, it was batted right out of my hand! . . . Sure . . . I remember . . . in your grandmother's house."

J.D. moved slowly up the stairs, first because he wasn't eager to go alone to his room with Blackbeard in the house; second, because he wanted to hear what his father said to Hank's father. At the top of the stairs he waited and listened.

"Same thing, huh?" said Mr. Jones. "I never would have believed it . . . Yeah . . . Took a big loss, eh? Well, I hope this thing doesn't drive us out of *our* place!"

Holy cow! thought J.D., what if our house got the reputation of being haunted! What if Blackbeard set it on fire! He took the first hesitant steps in the direction of his room. What if Dad keeps on insulting Blackbeard!

At the end of the hall where J.D.'s room was, it was pitch black, and it took a lot of courage to get there. He turned the knob as if it were a stick of dynamite, opened the door, and quickly crossed the darkened room to his dresser, upon which rested a small lamp. As he fumbled under the shade for the switch, his left hand came in contact with something cold lying on the dresser. It was hard and curved. Delicately, his fingers traveled along the surface until, with a shock of realization, he felt the hilt. It was Captain Teach's cutlass! He snapped on the light.

Fearfully, J.D. raised his eyes from the cutlass to the large mirror above the dresser. He could see how white his face was, as his eyes traveled from one side of the mirror to the other. He heaved a sigh of relief.

*If I can see his sword, I should be able to see him! Maybe he really* ain't *here; maybe he went over to Hank's.* These were his thoughts as he studied the reflection of the room in the mirror. To his right was his lumpy overstuffed armchair; behind it, the book-cases, and on the walls his pennants and pic-

tures. Everything was in its place, and no
Blackbeard.

Relieved, J.D. turned away from the mirror,
only to suck in a startled "Uhhhhhh!"

Invisible in the mirror, but plainly visible
to J.D.'s eyes, the ghost of Captain Teach
lounged deep within the cozy confines of the
easy chair, booted feet spread wide. His coat
collar was bunched high about his neck, hat
pulled low over his forehead. Filling all the
space between was bushy black beard. All
J.D. could see that resembled a face were two
uneven rows of grinning yellow teeth and one
amused glowing eye. Blackbeard's arms hung
limply over the sides of the chair, one hand
loosely holding the bottle of rum.

J.D. leaped for the door. His hand was on
the knob when he heard the deep voice rumble, "Hold on, me bucko!"

J.D. froze.

"C'mon in and set."

Something about the voice was both reassuring and disarming. Taking a deep breath,
J.D. turned and faced the pirate. Teach was
smiling broadly. Ghost or no ghost, thought
J.D., he doesn't look or act like one. But why
is it that sometimes people can hear him, then
other times not? And why is it only Hank and
I can see him, and then only part of the time?

J.D.'s conception of a ghost was a skeleton
wrapped in a sheet, who went about dragging
chains and moaning. Blackbeard didn't at all
fill that description.

"No sense in fearing good ol' honest Cap'n Teach! Set yourself down, lad." He spoke as if the room belonged to him. J.D. backed toward his bed and sat as far from Teach as he could, his eyes moving in wonder from Teach to the mirror and back to Teach again.

The burly pirate pushed his hat back on his head, scowled, and waved the bottle in the direction of the mirror. "That blasted looking glass won't work for me nohow! Bloody shame, 'tis!" He put the bottle to his lips, raised it high, and it gurgled. Then making a wry face, he wiped his mouth on his sleeve. "Ol' Teach ain't seen himself in years."

For a while he was silent and J.D. fidgeted nervously. Then Blackbeard held the bottle to the light, squinted at it with one eye, turned it upside down and, convinced it was empty, placed it with a long sigh on the floor beside his chair.

"This here town," he complained, "ain't what it used to be, but it be a heap better'n where I was!"

There was another silence, this time much longer, during which he warily studied J.D. The boy felt as though he were some kind of a specimen under the microscope of a madman on a TV thriller. Finally Teach spoke. "When are ye fixing to send me back, lad? Ye know I be overstaying my leave. Effen I be late getting back ol' Teach can get into a peck o' trouble with that red swab down there!" He pumped a big thumb at the floor. "Horns like a cow, he has!" Resting his elbows on his knees, he leaned forward. "Ye *are* planning to send Teach back, ain't ye?"

J.D. heard himself speak in a voice that seemed miles away. "That's . . . that's just it . . . sir . . . I don't know *how* to send you back!"

With an incredulous stare, Teach rose from the chair and paced the floor. "Hmmnnnn," he said thoughtfully, "now that be a pretty kettle of fish!" Then he turned a beaming face on J.D. "But I say now, lad, don't let hit worry ye none . . . me being docked close by the Boar's Head, and all."

He again pointed at the floor. "But, by all the bones in Davy's Locker, effen I don't *ever* get back . . . !" His laugh was a roar, and he used his dirty handkerchief to wipe the tears of mirth from his eyes. At any minute J.D. expected to hear his parents' rapid foot-steps. He was positive that not only they but everyone in the block must have heard the explosive laughter. He eyed the door and waited.

Blackbeard stuffed the rag back into his pocket. "You're sure now, lad?" he said, spear-ing a thick finger at J.D. "Ye be sure for *sartin* ye don't know how to send a body back?"

"Cross my heart, Captain Teach!"

The pirate turned away from J.D., and with his hands clasped behind his back, crossed to the window and studied the Joneses' yard. He spoke over his shoulder, spacing his words carefully and slyly. "And . . . effen ye *could* send me back" — he wheeled and faced J.D. — "what then, lad, what *then?*"

"Oh, no, *no sir!*" J.D. blurted. "I'll only do what you want me to . . . sir!"

Blackbeard heaved a great rumbling sigh of satisfaction, and a grin of triumph spread over his features. "Well now, J.D., lad, that be just fine, I say. And I takes it right hearty what ye did for ol' Teach, I does. Mark'ee, from this day on, ol' Teach and J.D. ships as mates, we do!" He moved his huge, ungainly frame to the dresser, scowled into the mirror, then turned a mournful face to J.D. He looked like a sheep dog who had just lost the sheep.

"But a blinking shame, 'tis, Cap'n Teach ashore, and nary a swab can see him . . . 'cept ye and Hank, that is." Turning to the mirror again, he peered into it regretfully. "And when ye figgers on all the poor, unlucky wenches what can't see ol' Teach!" He heaved a melancholy sigh. "It sure battens down me hatches, it do!" Shuffling to the chair, he sank heavily into it.

J.D. actually felt sorry for him. "Jeepers," he said sympathetically, "I'm sorry, Captain." His eyes lit up. "We could try it again . . . maybe this time . . ."

Teach exploded! "Try it again? Not on your life, lad! Ye'd have me back down there afore you could say 'Ol' Bailey'!"

The pirate sat and pondered. At last he raised his chin from the two hamlike fists that supported it, and asked with a note of suspicion in his voice, "Who were the witch, lad? Who were the witch whose ashes ye used to write the magic marks in?"

"Ashes?" J.D. exclaimed. "I didn't use ashes; I used flour."

Teach sat erect. "*Flour?*" he gasped. "Ye mean the stuff ye bake bread with?"

"Yes sir."

With a small whimper, Blackbeard fell weakly back into the chair. "Gor blimey!" he said to the ceiling. "He used *flour!*" His beard came down upon his chest. Incredulous and amazed, he asked, "Didn't ye know, lad, you're s'posed to use the ashes of a witch new-burned at the stake?"

J.D. studied and picked at a fingernail. "No sir," he mumbled.

"So that be why the wenches don't have the pleasure o' seeing ol' Teach! And I have to split a tops'l, else ye lads wouldn't see me, neither!" He got up and, clasping his hands behind his back, paced the room again.

"Effen ye couldn't get a witch, why in thunder didn't ye get the ashes o' a couple o' toads, or a snake or two . . . burned at ye dark o' the moon, o' course?" He stopped pacing and scratched his head. "Nope, wouldn'ta worked, neither. For the wenches you're needing a real witch." His brow furrowed in deep thought; then he wheeled to face J.D. "Ye wouldn't be knowing the where-abouts o' a real live witch now, would ye, lad? We could . . ."

The thought horrified J.D. "Oh, no! No sir!"

Teach hopelessly synchronized the shaking of his head with J.D.'s "No witches, huh?" He turned away, then back again, his little finger digging into a hairy ear. "You're *sure* there ain't a live witch in Godolphin Town?"

J.D. nodded vigorously. "Yes sir, I'm sure, sir!"

Teach frowned. "How in blazes can a town get along without a witch?" he muttered, eas-ing himself into the heavy chair. "What do a body do, effen a body catches the gout, or the ague, or a boil, even?" For a while the room was silent, with both of them staring despon-dently at the floor. Then suddenly Teach looked up. "What is this bilge, lad, about tearing down me Boar's Head?"

"They're going to build a gas station, sir."

"A gas station?"

"Yes sir."

"Tell me, lad, what be a blooming gas sta-tion?"

"It's a place where people buy gas and oil, and stuff for their cars."

"Ye mean to feed them grunting wagons what go by themself, 'thout a horse a-pulling?"

"Yes sir."

The pirate's beard bristled, and he scowled in unbelieving scorn. "And for *that* they be fixing to scuttle the finest taproom in the Colonies?"

"Yes sir, I guess so, sir."

Blackbeard wiped his nose on his sleeve. "Aye," he said slowly, "they must be daft!" He paused, frowning. "Who, lad, who be the swab what *thinks* he owns me Boar's Head?"

J.D. answered hesitantly, "Uh . . . uh . . . Mr. Maynard, sir."

It was as though Teach had been shot out of a cannon. J.D. went flat on his back across the studio couch and scrambled into the corner. The pirate grabbed his cutlass from the dresser and stalked to the bed.

"Be ye for sartin that scurvy swab's name be *Maynard?*" he thundered.

J.D.'s jaw worked.

"Speak up, lad, speak up!" Teach bellowed. "Be the wonk's name Maynard?"

"Y-y-y-y yessir!"

"Why, that scurvy bit o' lead-swinging gawpus!" He howled and stormed up and down the room. "Owns me Boar's Head, do he? Why, I fit 'gators with me bare hands, I did . . . chawed the living gizzard out o' any swab that stood agin me!" He glared at J.D. "I were a murdering, gouging sea shark, I were!"

Then, to J.D.'s surprise, he abruptly turned his back on the boy and bowed his head in shame and disgust. "And what happens? I get meself scuttled by that lily-livered shrimp Maynard!" When Teach again faced J.D., the boy was startled to see actual tears in his eyes, and when he spoke, it was with mingled hurt and indignation. "Stabbed me in the back, he did! Stabbed me in the back. Done me in just when kind and gentle ol' Teach were feeding vittles to some poor starving orphins."

He walked slowly to the dresser, put down his cutlass, removed his handkerchief, and blew his nose. Then he went to the window and looked up at the sky and sniffed once or twice. Looking over his shoulder at J.D., he assumed a wheedling tone. "But . . . d'ye s'pose, J.D., lad, this be the *same* sly, thieving, backstabbing Maynard what done in friendly ol' Teach? The Maynard what done *me* in was a big strong feller about so high." He held his hand a foot above his head.

J.D. answered quickly, relieved that Teach was himself again. "Oh no, sir!" he said with emphasis. "This is a different Mr. Maynard. Pop Allan, our history teacher, who knows all about pirates and stuff, says this Mr. Maynard is a descendant, or something. He says this Mr. Maynard is a worse robber than . . . than . . . uh . . ."

Teach's eyes were cold as he came around, and the boy, after a few hard swallows, continued. "The old Captain Maynard got the Boar's Head from Governor Eden for killing . . . killing . . ." J.D. gulped and wondered why he had ever opened his big mouth. Then he blurted, "It's been in his family ever since . . . sir."

Blackbeard scowled in disbelief. "Ye be telling Teach that lump o' hog blubber Eden give me Boar's Head to Maynard? For doing me in?" J.D. cringed and in horror watched the pirate pull an ugly knife from his belt. "I be coming for ye, Eden!" he snarled. Halfway across the room he paused, screwed up his face, and scratched his cheek. "Blast Eden!" he mumbled to himself. "Can't be hurting a ghost!" He turned helplessly to J.D., who wondered at the reason for the sudden change.

"This Maynard feller," Teach queried, "he be o' Maynard blood, be'n't he? Big feller, too, I reckon." J.D. nodded and Teach shoved his knife back into his belt. "Aye, lad, mayhap we better sleep on it. 'Twill be time enow on the morrow to careen Maynard's scurvy hulk."

Yawning, he removed his pistols, knife, and belt, placed them on the dresser beside the cutlass, and removed his jacket. Scratching his back, Teach looked around the room for a place to hang his coat. On the door was a hook and a clothes hanger. He took the hanger down and, with a puzzled look, inspected it carefully before tossing it aside and hanging the coat on the hook.

Next, he shuffled to the dresser, scratching his ribs, picked up a pistol and his cutlass, turned to the bed, sat down, and kicked off his boots. J.D. stared in astonishment and quickly left the entire bed to the pirate, who stretched out, pistol in one hand, cutlass in the other.

He squinted at the priming of his pistol and said, "Never can tell 'bout that Maynard swab!"

Yawning, he pointed at the window with his cutlass. "Batten down ye hatches, lad, and secure the ports. Night air be mighty unhealthful!" Then, crossing hairy arms upon his chest, a weapon in each hand, he closed his eyes and immediately began to snore.

The Joneses' back screen door creaked a rusty sound as it was carefully opened and closed, and a wash of moonlight revealed J.D. descending the steps to the back yard. Above him a shutter moved in a slow, easy arc, thumped once against the wall, and was still.

J.D. hesitated and threw a quick glance upward. Then he hurried down the steps, crossed the moving patch of moonlight, and vaulted the low fence that divided the Jones and Oberteuffer properties. Stumbling over a toy wagon and ducking under the branches of an apple tree, he crouched like a hunted jackal below Hank's first-floor bedroom window. He darted a look up at his own window. The shutter wavered, undecided.

Selecting a few small pebbles, he tossed them against the screen of Hank's open window, and Butch barked. It seemed like an age before Hank's groggy face appeared between the curtains, his fist rubbing a sleepy eye. "Hey!" said Hank into the night. "What's up?"

"It's me — J.D. He's in my room!"

"Who's in your room?"

"Who? Who else, ya jerk, the *ghost!*"

Hank forced his eyes upward toward J.D.'s window. "Ohmigosh!" he breathed.

J.D. rose to his feet. "Lemme in, will ya? I'm not staying in that house tonight!"

"Sure, sure, go around to the back door."

In Hank's room, shoulder to shoulder, the two boys peered at the upstairs window. Black tree shadows writhed over the clapboards. The loose shutter slammed a few times to attract attention, then waved like a beckoning hand. The fur on Butch's back bristled, he growled once, and then with tail between his legs, crept under the bed. J.D. grabbed Hank's arm. "Hank!" he gasped. "What'll we do?"

# 3: MONDAY

# 10

IF YOU FOLLOWED J.D. and Hank up Elm Street, as Captain Teach was doing, you would find that it led directly to the entrance to Godolphin Junior High School.

J.D. had sneaked into the house before his parents were up. His mother was pleasantly shocked, when she entered the kitchen to find him doing a last bit of checking on his home-work and eating a bowlful of cereal. It was J.D.'s turn to be shocked when he jogged down the front steps.

" 'Morning to ye, J.D., lad," boomed Captain Teach.

He was standing on the sidewalk right in front of the house! J.D. gulped, " 'Morning," and sped diagonally across the lawn toward

Hank, who was three houses up the block, hiding behind a tree. Together, after an exchange of worried looks, they proceeded at a faster pace than usual toward what they hoped would be the safety of the school.

Teach rolled along fifty feet behind them, gaining rapidly. Butch kept pace with the boys, trotting down the center of the street, his tail between his legs, now and then casting a furtive glance at Teach.

"Is he still there?" asked J.D.

Hank took a quick look over his shoulder. "Yeah," he said. "You know, J.D., I still can't figure out why nobody can see him except us . . . and Butch."

"That's easy; we used flour."

"Flour?"

Hank looked puzzled. "What has flour got to do with it?"

J.D. shifted his books to the other arm. "We're the only ones that can see him because we used flour instead of the ashes of a witch burned at the stake."

Hank gave J.D. a long, suspicious stare. "Hang loose, J.D., who are you kidding?"

"I'm not kidding. That's why nobody can see him except us . . . and then only when he wants us to. He told me!"

Hank took another quick look over his shoulder at Teach, and then back at J.D. "You mean *him*?"

"Yeah."

Teach noted the gesture, waved gaily, and almost stumbled over a root projecting from the sidewalk.

Godolphin Junior High was a large red brick and stone structure surrounded by low hedges and a bit of frazzled lawn. J.D. and Hank, closely followed by Blackbeard, twisted their way between the groups of students gathered about the entrance. Skirting the low hedge, they found themselves blocked by three husky high school seniors, each wearing an identical sweater with a large letter "G" on the front. They recognized Judy's big brother, the star fullback, and behind him, the star right guard and tackle of the football team. All of them were grinning in a way that both J.D. and Hank knew could mean trouble.

"How's the spook business, J.D.?" grinned the tackle.

"Yeah," sneered the right guard, "seen any ghosts lately, Hank?"

Judy's brother drew himself up to his full six feet, closed his eyes, and moaned, "Oh . . . Captain Teach . . . you crummy old ghost, come to us!"

"Aw, cut it out, you guys," said J.D. He tried to pass, but was blocked by all three. Their fun had just started!

"Oh . . . Blackbeard!" cried the star fullback, his eyes still tightly shut, but he never finished. Like lightning, an invisible hand yanked his tie from his sweater and gave it a tremendous jerk, pulling him forward, off balance, so that he almost fell. His eyes opened. He paused for a second, then snorted angrily, "Okay, you . . .!" and lunged savagely at J.D.

It was as if he had charged into an oncoming locomotive. Back he went over the hedge, taking his two friends with him.

The idols of the Godolphin football squad slowly sat up, ten feet beyond the hedge, and stared in astonishment at the backs of J.D. and Hank as they passed between the parting ranks of wondering students.

The long, dim corridor on the main floor of the school was lined with metal lockers painted a bilious green. At intervals of forty feet or so were the classroom doors. The students milled along in an undulating two-way stream, five hundred shuffling feet creating the background for a constant babble and chatter of voices, punctuated by the frequent slam of locker doors.

J.D. and Hank's first class of the day was located at the far end of the corridor, and with Captain Teach close at their heels, they worked their way through the human maelstrom.

"The orphin asylum sure has growed," Teach muttered through his beard. "This *new* Maynard feller must be a mean un, all right."

Suddenly, from everywhere, came an ear-splitting, shattering clanging of electric bells, and from the throat of Blackbeard rose a screech of fear. Whipping out his cutlass, he crashed back against the lockers, his body taut. The students scattered, and the doorways sucked them out of sight. By the time the bells stopped ringing, the hall was deserted.

There was absolute silence and Teach crouched, scowling, on widespread feet, cutlass thrust forward, ready for any emergency. As the silence continued, he moved cautiously to the center of the hall and, in slow motion, turned a puzzled full circle. "What in blazes scared them young-uns?" he said to himself.

The door behind him swooshed open, and he whipped around to face the new danger. The point of his cutlass was inches from the delectable figure of Miss Deedee Hooker, art teacher, as she paused and scrutinized a small notebook held in her hand. Blackbeard's bushy eyebrows arched high, and his lips formed the tiny opening necessary for an admiring whistle. The point of the cutlass descended.

Miss Hooker knit her lovely brow and, with the end of a pencil, tapped her even white teeth. Sheathing his cutlass, Blackbeard, hands clasped behind him, head cocked to one side, strolled completely around Miss Deedee, studying her with as much delight as if she were a chest filled with newly acquired gold.

She drew a deep breath, exhaled impatiently through red lips, tucked the pencil into her hair and swept down the hall. Teach's eyes devoured her dainty figure. Then, giving his pants a hitch, he rolled and lurched in pursuit.

The last period of the school day was nearing its end, and in Room 148 Mr. George Allan, teacher of history, was winding up a lecture on "Pirates and Piracy in Colonial America," a subject on which he was an authority.

Mr. Allan was also winding up forty-five years of a dedicated teaching career. His tall, gangling, tweedy figure would be sadly missed in the corridors and classrooms of Godolphin Junior High. Many years before, when he graduated from a small Midwestern college, the thought of teaching school was as remote to him as the savage and distant places he intended to explore. His life would be an adventure! He would become a scholarly vagabond of sea and jungle — write books about it.

Allan had worked his way to the South Seas aboard a tramp steamer. In Papeete, moored at the dock, was a sloop with sails like the wings of a gull, so rigged that one man could easily handle her, and for sale at a bargain price. But one night, just before the sale was consummated, his carefully planned career melted like butter.

He met her on the beach, and there was a moon. She was a nurse and traveling companion for a wealthy widow, and both ladies came from Godolphin, North Carolina.

The purchase price of the sloop went, instead, into the down payment of a small house in Godolphin, and George Allan, adventurer, became George Allan, teacher.

As long as he lived, he never once regretted this decision. The marriage was a long and happy one. But now, each Sunday found him standing beside the grave of the one he had met on that island so long ago, and for whom he had sacrificed the carefree life of a wanderer.

He never did see those far-off places, or watch masses of white clouds pile up over lonely, deserted islands, yet people got the impression that he had.

Vigorous outdoor living during the long summer vacations had bronzed his leathery skin. Time had turned his unruly shock of hair to iron gray, and plowed deep furrows into his cheeks and neck. He was lean and hard, and walked and talked like Trader Horn. He knew more about sea and jungle and all those other wonderful things than any man in town.

George Allan looked, acted, and spoke like everything he was not.

If the subject of his lecture happened to be a dry topic of history, he warmed it with interesting anecdotes, polishing it off with a fabulous yarn that had every student in the class hanging on his words until the dismissal bell. On the way out there was always a noisy cluster lingering around his desk. Everyone called him Pop.

Now, in Room 148, the afternoon sun painted Pop Allan's face and neck a glowing red. He stood between his desk and a tripod easel upon which was displayed a large picture in color of Captain Kidd. Waving a sheaf of papers in the direction of the portrait, he said, "Of the pirates we have studied so far, Captain Kidd is, of course, the most famous, but he was a mere babe in arms in comparison with our next example."

He leafed through a few prints on his desk, then turned to the class and grinned, "Just wait until you get a load of *this* character!"

Noises of anticipation came from his audience, and Hank took advantage of the situation to whisper to J.D., who sat in front of him. "Did you see him in any of your classes, J.D."

"I ain't seen him all day, but that don't mean anything!"

Hank's eyes moved from side to side and he whispered, "Did you hear about all the funny stuff that went on in Miss Hooker's classes? She went home early."

"Yeah, I heard. Do you suppose it was . . . ? Holy cow! It must have been!"

Hank nudged J.D. and nodded toward Allan, who was holding aloft a large engraved portrait of Captain Teach.

"Oh *no!*" J.D. breathed.

"What do you think of this fellow?" Allan smiled. There was a whoop of enthusiasm from the class.

In the picture, Blackbeard, armed to the teeth and scowling as usual, was standing on a strip of beach with the *Queen Anne's Revenge* in the background. Allan placed the print over that of Captain Kidd and said, "Handsome fellow, wasn't he?" Again came a whoop of laughter, but not from J.D. nor Hank; their horrified gaze was fixed on the area behind the desk where Teach was doing a fade-in! He waved and grinned at the boys.

"This," said Allan, pointing at the print, "is Captain Edward Teach, better known as Blackbeard, the most daring and colorful pirate of them all."

And there he actually was, looming like an immense monolith, dwarfing Allan, his face flushed with pleasure. Hank's eyes were like two smoke-filled glass balls; he looked as if he had just been shot. J.D.'s stomach slowly revolved.

The pirate grinned, jabbed a thumb at the picture, then at his chest, and struck the same pose. Allan continued. "On the other hand, his name might have been Thatch. History is not quite clear on that." Blackbeard violently shook his head no, and plunked himself into Allan's swivel chair behind the desk.

Allan spoke glowingly of the pirate's escapades, and Blackbeard's dark scowl changed to a shy smile, his eyes sparkled, and he leaned eagerly forward, elbows on desk, hands clasped before him, head nodding agreement. Allan

waved his notes toward the portrait. "Teach,"
he said, "was really the greatest of them all.
He was a pirate's pirate — a terror on land as
well as sea."

Teach proudly flashed a grin at the boys,
pumped a thumb at his chest, and again turned
his attention back to Allan.

"He was an enormous and powerful man,"
the teacher went on. "When he went into a sea
battle, he tied cannon fuses into his beard and
ignited them." He pointed at the picture.
"That's where all that smoke comes from. He
must have scared the living daylights out of
everyone. I personally wouldn't want to get
near him. Believe me, this fellow played
rough!"

Blackbeard was so pleased he actually
blushed. Glancing at J.D., his eyes said, "Aw
. . . I warn't that good!" and he hung his
head like an embarrassed schoolboy.

"But," Allan added, "without a doubt, Edward Teach was just about as vicious, evil,
and nasty a scoundrel as ever lived . . . with
or without the smoke effects."

J.D. and Hank watched in horror as Blackbeard, his face a thundercloud, rose from the
chair to stand glowering down on Allan, who
had sat down in the chair the instant Teach
left it. The pirate's storm of wrath had reached
a crescendo; and Pop Allan, warming to his
subject, continued as Hank slipped lower and
lower in his seat, his face like chalk.

"Not only that," said Allan, "he was the worst . . ." He paused and studied Hank. "Henry, are you all right?"

Teach was drawing his cutlass, but he, too, paused and eyed the boy with concern. Hank blinked.

"Huh?" he said.

"Are you all right?"

Hank's eyes began to focus again, and he saw Allan and Teach, standing side by side, both viewing him with anxiety. He swallowed hard a few times. "Sure, sure," he squeaked, "I'm okay."

"If you don't feel well . . ."

The look Hank cast at Teach was like the one Butch used when he begged for a bone. Then he turned his eyes to the mystified Allan, who glanced at the place where Teach stood, then back at the boy. Hank said weakly, "No . . . I feel fine, sir!"

"Well . . ." He stopped and looked steadily at the boy for a moment. There was something strange going on, and he wondered what it was. He glanced down at the notes on his desk and said, "Well, let's see, where was I?" He moved papers, crumpled one and threw it into the wastebasket, looked at his watch, and got up out of the chair. He walked around to the front of his desk and sat down on the edge of it, looking over his glasses at the class.

"I am afraid," he said, "we are running out of time. I guess we'll have to finish off Blackbeard tomorrow."

Teach stabbed Allan with a sharp look.

"But I do have time to say a few things about Teach and the Boar's Head Tavern. Some of you perhaps know this fine old building was built by Blackbeard, and he lived there for a while. Eventually, however, the planters and the townspeople had all they could take from Teach and Company. Knowing very well their own Governor Eden wouldn't cooperate with them, they appealed to Governor Spotswood of Virginia."

Allan ambled to the blackboard and, as he spoke, drew a rough map of Pamlico Sound in the Godolphin and Ocracoke area. "One fine morning two ships set sail in search of Teach and his crew, who were doing a little pirating near Ocracoke Inlet."

The smouldering Captain Teach was standing behind Allan and, with much curiosity, watched the map being drawn. His hands were clasped behind his back and his legs spread wide. "The Captain," said Allan, "of the first sloop to make contact with Teach's vessel was a man whose name is familiar to us all — Robert Maynard." He finished the map and turned to face the class, Blackbeard's burning eyes followed his every move.

"A battle took place, and Teach and most of his crew were wiped out."

Blackbeard shook his head sadly, and turned a doleful face to the boys. He drew his handkerchief from his pocket and blew his nose as he watched Allan draw a large cross on the map.

"It was on this spot," said Allan, pointing at the cross he had drawn, "that contact was made with Teach's ship, and the frightful battle took place." He laid the chalk down and, brushing the dust from his hands, walked to the front of his desk and sat, while Teach planted himself in front of the map and studied it carefully with much back-scratching and grunting.

The teacher waved his notes nonchalantly in the direction of Teach and the map. "It took a lot of men with courage to rid the earth of this dangerous wolf-of-the-sea." Teach gave Allan a swift nod of thanks, then turned back to the map. "And the people of Godolphin were so delighted, they and Governor Eden gave Maynard the Boar's Head Tavern. Personally, though, I don't think he earned it. History shows that Blackbeard was half dead before Maynard tackled him!" Teach nodded again.

"The old building has been in the Maynard family ever since, but now it has been sold, and at this very moment this fine example of early American architecture is being torn down." Blackbeard slowly came round with one bushy eyebrow raised and the other a lowering black clump that almost covered his eye. Allan blithely continued with his talk.

"I had hoped that one day this venerable old house might be turned into a museum of early Americana. I planned to donate my collection of pirate lore, if only the city would buy and take over the building, but our town miser, Joe Maynard, insisted on such an exorbitant price for the place the city couldn't afford it."

Teach was hanging on every work Allan said. His beard was smoking furiously. Then, as J.D. and Hank goggled, he grew hazy, and vanished. Only the strong acrid smell of burning gunpowder told them he was still in the room.

From the mouths of the students Allan heard gasps of amazement as three dozen pairs of eyes stared in astonishment. They were watching a piece of chalk that had jumped up behind him and was dancing about like a cork on rough water. With bated breath, the children saw it prance and frolic up to the blackboard and hover over the map. Then the gyrations of the chalk began again. An invisible hand rubbed out Allan's cross and vigorously redrew it with a new location. Then, in a graceful arc, the chalk made its exit through the open window.

The swivel chair whirled like a dervish. The classroom door opened violently and, slamming shut, seemed to trigger the clanging of the dismissal bell.

# 11

Hᴀɴᴋ, despite his previous stonelike aspect, was halfway down the hall before the dismissal bell stopped ringing. Now he waited for J.D. at their usual meeting place behind an old frame building adjacent to the athletic field.

A couple of chattering girls passed, each hugging a stack of books to her chest. Hank viewed them indifferently, wondering, "Why do girls always have to lug so many books home? They don't get any more homework to do than we do."

One of the girls exclaimed, "I tell you, Sophie, it just *must* have been a ghost . . . a *real* ghost too!" This comment jolted Hank's thoughts back to the tormenting problems of

Captain Teach. He lowered his head and kicked at the cinders.

J.D. had lagged behind in the mad exodus from the classroom. Maybe, he thought, Pop Allan might know what to do. He thought about the coming night. Sooner or later his parents would find out that he wasn't sleeping in his room. The likely chance that he might be forced to sleep in the same room with the ghost was too horrible even to imagine. It was this last thought that made him stop in the doorway and look back at his teacher.

The elderly man was moving in a dazed manner toward his desk. He dropped into his chair, took out his handkerchief, and cleaned his eyeglasses as he blinked vaguely at the notes on his desk.

J.D. drifted into the room. "Pop . . . could I . . . ?"

Allan raised his face. "Hm?" he said, and looked at J.D. as if he had never seen him before. He adjusted his glasses and looked over them at the boy. "Oh . . . J.D.," he said vaguely.

"Pop . . . I . . ."

"Yes?"

The words lurched from J.D.'s mouth. "It's just that I've got to tell you something. I . . ."

"Tell me something?"

"About the chalk, sir . . . the crazy chalk."

Allan's brow puckered, and he gave the boy an intense look. He waved a hand toward the blackboard. "You mean you know something about that?"

J.D. hung his head. "Yes, sir."

Allan's eyes widened. The boy's lip twitched, but no sound came. For the first time Allan became impatient with a student. "Well, tell me!" he snapped. "Don't just stand there!"

The words tumbled out. "It's just that Blackbeard was right here in this room all the time you were talking, sir! And it's my fault!"

"Blackbeard? You mean the pirate?"

"Yes sir. Captain Teach. Hank and me, we ..."

"You mean *Edward* Teach?"

"Yes sir. It's my fault, sir. Hank and me ..."

"*Your* fault? What do you mean your fault? What did you do?"

J.D. lifted a tortured face. "It was his ghost that wrote that stuff on the blackboard — Captain Teach's ghost. And I was the one that bought him back. He's apt to do anything, Pop! He could even hurt somebody!"

Pop Allan eyed J.D. skeptically. Then he laughed in a reassuring way. "Nonsense, my boy! Ghosts don't exist!"

"Oh yes, they do! They certainly do! At least Blackbeard's does."

Allan dubiously pursed his lips and glanced at the inscription on the blackboard. "Fantastic!" he murmured. "Fantastic!" He squinted at J.D. "But why," he asked, "do you think it's your fault? How in the world could you have brought him back?"

"That was easy, Pop. Hank and I were over at the Boar's Head and we found this old paper in a hole down in the dungeon under the . . ."

"Dungeon? Where was the dungeon?"

"Under the Boar's Head. We . . ."

"You mean to tell me there is a cellar under that place?"

"Yes sir."

Allan looked vacantly at the floor and rubbed his chin as J.D. continued. "And we found . . . *this*." From his notebook he drew forth the now flattened document. Mechanically, Allan took off his glasses, cleaned them, replaced them, and inspected the yellowed parchment with great curiosity. "Amazing!" he muttered.

J.D. pointed at the parchment. "We tried it, sir, and it worked! But it was me that brought back the ghost. It was my idea to have a seance. Hank was against it from the start. But holy cow, Pop, how did I know it would work? I thought it was a gag!"

Allan's voice was hushed with awe. "You mean you uttered these words . . . and it materialized this . . . this specter?"

"Yes sir. Only that ain't all. I drew those funny marks in some flour I sprinkled on the table."

"Flour?"

"Yes sir. But I should have used the ashes of a witch new-burned at the stake. It works better that way," he said with authority.

"Incredible!" Allan breathed, "Absolutely incredible!"

His teacher's reception of his confession reassured J.D. He felt much better now; Pop was on his side. "Nobody can see him 'cept Hank and me," he announced.

Allan's head came up, startled. "You say you can actually *see* the thing? You saw it today? In this classroom?"

"Sure! Me and Hank see him practically all the time. I talk with him a lot too. You know, he's a pretty nice guy . . . for a ghost. But we can't see him all the time, because, like I said, I drew the magic marks in flour, instead of using the ashes of a dead witch. If I did that, everybody could see him." He backed toward the door. "Could I go now, Pop?"

Allan vacantly nodded his assent, turning empty eyes back to the parchment. "Ashes from a dead witch," he muttered. "Good Lord!"

J.D. edged through the doorway and clattered down the halls and out of the building.

Across the athletic field, a little beyond the fence that surrounded it, a young woman pushed a baby carriage beneath spring-green foliage, over a carpeting of dappled sunlight and shadow. In a far corner of the grounds, on the spot where once, long ago, the gallows had stood, a few boys played baseball, and their distant cries mingled with the chirping of birds.

J.D. raced toward the place where Hank was impatiently waiting. To amuse himself Hank was pressing his back tightly against the wall of a storage shed, trying to see how far out he could extend his feet without slipping to the ground. He was so absorbed in this endeavor that he didn't notice J.D. turn the corner of the building.

"I told Pop," J.D. called.

Hank's feet scrabbled wildly in the cinders, then he slid to the ground with a thump. "Jeepers!" he complained. "Why don't you give a guy a warning? I thought you were that crummy ghost!" He picked up his book. "What took you so long?"

"I was talking to Pop."

"What about?"

"The ghost. I told him what happened."

"Yeah? What did he say? Did he get sore?"

"Naw," J.D. drawled, "he got all excited about it."

"Jeepers!"

The boys headed across the almost deserted athletic field toward the gate in the iron fence. Because of his talk with Allan, J.D.'s fears had largely evaporated. Pop was on his side now, and that was good enough insurance for anybody. Unfortunately, this new-found courage did not extend itself to Hank.

They heard the sharp *dok!* of wood striking hard leather, and a ball soared through the air, curving foul away from the diamond. It hit the ground not far from where they stood, bounced a few times, and rolled toward the boys. Both lunged for it. In the scuffle, Hank emerged the victor, and heaved a long throw back to the diamond. He turned to J.D. and his wide, freckled grin sickened and died on his lips. Ten feet beyond his friend stood Blackbeard!

Hank's face paled and his body went stiff. J.D. did an about-face, knowing full well who would be there. Hank ripped into action, but J.D. grabbed his wrist before he could get away.

The expression on Blackbeard's face was terrifying. It was a ghastly grin, half smirk and half leer, and his eyes glittered with deadly menace. The burning fuses in his beard sputtered and oozed gobs of acrid-smelling smoke. Occasionally his face would be hidden within this smog, then gradually it would reappear, like a diabolical full moon from behind a cloud.

Teach drew his cutlass. "Ho, me lad, I be a-waiting for ye!" he rumbled. "Are ye with ol' Teach? Are ye going to help tear the gullet outten that lily-livered slobgollion Maynard?"

J.D.'s grip tightened on Hank's wrist. He nodded his head. "Yes sir."

"That's the pepper, lads!" Jabbing his cutlass aloft, Teach slowly drew back his clenched fist and lunged a finger in the direction of the Boar's Head Tavern. "Then forward, men!" he roared. "Give the swabs a taste o' our steel!" And he resolutely marched toward the gate. "Tear down me Boar's Head, will ye?" he thundered. "Not while Blackbeard be on deck, ye won't!"

These words washed away some of J.D.'s new-found valor, and for a moment he hesitated. But the thought of Pop, and the fact that Teach could do someone bodily harm, sparked him into action. He started after Teach, dragging his unwilling ally with him. In a near whisper he rasped, "C'mon!"

Hank jerked his wrist loose from the clutching hand, rubbed it, and flipped an angry look at J.D. "I'm not following that . . . that . . . guy!" he protested. "Think I'm crazy?"

"Look," J.D. pleaded, "we don't actually have to go with him. Just follow him! We've got to warn Maynard! Teach could kill the guy! You don't want to be responsible for that, do you? We'd get blamed for it. We could even get put in jail!" He put his hand on Hank's arm.

Hank snapped his arm away and retreated a few paces. "Well . . . I'll go with you, J.D., but," he added quickly, "I won't go near him!"

"Okay, you don't have to. You don't think for a minute I'm going to get near him, do you? . . . Aw, c'mon, Hank!" and Hank reluctantly came.

Puffing and blowing, J.D. sprinted out of Spotswood Avenue into Main Street. He looked tensely up and down the wide thoroughfare, then back at his balky friend, who was finally making it to the corner where J.D. stood, just two blocks from the Boar's Head. From down Main Street came the familiar deep, trumpeting voice of Captain Teach. "After 'em," they heard him bellow, "ye mangy rum-loving scallywags! A hundred pieces o' eight extra for the swab that hands ol' Teach the gizzard outten that belly-robbing guarro Maynard!"

Hank and J.D.'s eyes met in alarm, both minds touched with the same thought. J.D. grasped Hank's wrist. Mechanically Hank disengaged the offending hand, and backing away, found refuge behind a newsstand. Teach sounded as if he were goading his entire gang of pirates into action!

Holy cow, thought J.D., has Pop started monkeying with that scroll already?

The booming voice of Blackbeard was growing louder as he drew near, and Hank and J.D. waited. Teach made a magnificent entrance. Brandishing his cutlass, he strode out from between a Dairy Queen Truck going north and a ratty station wagon going in the opposite direction. Apparently he was alone, and it was only force of habit that had prompted him to yell to his crew. J.D. expelled a sigh of relief.

The pirate barreled along, clumping up the white center line between streams of moving traffic, trailing smoke, and shouting as if he were in the midst of a sea battle.

J.D. and Hank watched as he swaggered up the street and out of sight. "Come on, Hank," called J.D., "we got the light," and he hurried across the street. Reaching the tavern, they found Teach standing on the gravel path leading to the house. Hands on hips, he was dubiously observing the activity around him.

Without taking his eyes from Blackbeard, J.D. said, "I'm going over by the gate. You coming?"

"Okay," Hank said bleakly. Then he added, "What do you suppose he's going to do?"

"Jeepers, I don't know!" Already they could feel the tension in the air. It was, J.D. thought, like watching the sputtering fire of a fuse inch toward a cherry bomb.

They watched a new Buick turn into the grounds, bump easily through the tall grass, and park near the truck. Its door opened and a florid man crawled out from behind the wheel. He squinted at the tavern, his fingers revolving the huge cigar in his mouth. He removed it, and a stream of smoke jetted from his thin lips. Blackbeard studied him suspiciously, then sauntered over to take a closer look at this character who bore a striking resemblance to Governor Eden.

A tanned and raw-boned figure in shirt sleeves filled the doorway of the Boar's Head. "Hi, Mr. Bailly," the man called, and jogged down the ramp. "Have a nice trip?"

Bailly scowled, and the smile on Jake's face turned to stone. "Don't tell me you're running into more trouble around here," Bailly growled. "Are you?"

"Nope, except like I said, nothing will come apart. Ain't been no more funny stuff, if that's what you mean."

Bailly spoke with his cigar clenched between his teeth. "What"s this stuff about expensive wood and ebony shingles? They look like ordinary shingles to me."

"You think you know ebony when you see it, boss?" Jake asked, and he pushed his tongue doubtfully against his cheek, viewing Bailly with something akin to disdain. Taking his time, he reached into a back pocket, withdrew a bit of shingle he had picked up earlier, and handed it to his boss. "The company's got a hundred thousand bucks worth of that kind of stuff in this shack!"

"What makes you so sure it's ebony?"

"So okay, don't believe me!"

"Hmmmnn," Bailly grunted. "Let's take a look."

The two men paraded up the ramp and into the house. "Holy cow, Hank!" J.D. breathed. "Do you think we should warn them?"

"You crazy?" Hank exploded. "In the first place, they'd say we were nuts. And in the second place, what if it got Blackbeard sore? You know what I think? I think we'd better get out of here, that's what I think!"

J.D.'s respect for Hank's opinion had improved. "Yeah," he said. "Maybe you're right."

"Right about what, J.D.?"

The familiar voice came from behind them. They turned and saw Pop Allan. "Right about what?" he repeated.

"It's Blackbeard, sir."

"You mean he's around here?" He nodded in the direction of the tavern. "Now?"

"Yes, sir. He's standing on the porch."

Allan rubbed his chin, and both boys were surprised at his impish smile. "I'll be doggoned!" he murmured. "Who would believe it?"

Within the taproom Bailly pompously poked about, picked up pieces of wood, examined them, and tossed them aside.

At the far end of the room, Jake lovingly stroked the timber that earlier had given so much trouble. It still remained in place. He patted it the way a used-car salesman pats the hood of a worn-out car. "Now, here's an ex-

ample, boss . . . solid chestnut. Take a look
for yourself." He faced Bailly. "Why, you
couldn't buy . . . Holy smoke, boss, what's the
matter?"

Bailly stood rigid as a post. His face was
ashen and his eyes bulged. Choking sounds
gurgled from his throat.

"Boss!" Jake yelled, and rushed to Bailly,
whose legs were crumbling under him. As
Bailly folded, Jake caught him in his arms,
and supported his staggering employer to the
porch, where he leaned against the wall gasping for breath. Jake scowled at the workmen
who had gathered. "Okay, you guys, Mr. Bailly
just had a little attack — something he et.
Nothing serious." His gesture ordered that
they move along. He turned to Bailly. "You
feel all right now, boss?"

"I guess so," Bailly gasped, as he massaged
his throat, the color of his face matching that
of the plaster rubble. "Jake," he asked hoarsely,
"did . . . did you see who was choking me?"

"Choking you? Nobody was choking you!"

Bailly glared at him. "What do you mean,
nobody was choking me? You think I didn't
feel his fingers around my neck?"

"I don't get it! You and me were the only
people in the room. Who could be choking
you?"

"A ghost, you idiot!"

"A ghost?" Jake's mouth hung wide.

Blackbeard, who had never left the porch,

grinned and waved to someone inside the house.

Bailly didn't carry the conversation further. Instead, he staggered down the ramp to his car. The door slammed, the motor roared, the spinning wheels grabbed sod and flung it far, as the car swerved between the trees. Entering Main Street, the tires squealed, and, after the motor's loud, savage growl melted into the distance, J.D. exclaimed, "Holy cow! Was that guy ever mad! Blackbeard must've done something!"

# 12

"I'm sorry, Miss Chadsey," Joe Maynard rasped in his high-pitched voice. "For the last time, I say it's out of the question." He selected several letters from the top of his desk, shuffled them into a neat pile and placed them in a top drawer. He leaned his lanky frame back in his swivel chair and closed his eyes; it wasn't so much a gesture of weariness as one of boredom.

"But, Mr. Maynard," the pretty girl pleaded, "my mother is too ill to be left alone! It would be just until I can get someone to stay with her. I'd only be gone for two days . . . or maybe less."

"No!"

The girl, stifling a sob, turned, put her handkerchief to her mouth, and fled to the door, which opened violently just as she reached for the knob.

As she left, J. M. Bailly stormed into the office. "Joe Maynard!" he yelled. "What kind of a stunt are you trying to pull?" Maynard's eyes popped open. "If you want to continue doing business with the Summit Oil Company, you'll tear up that contract and give us our money back, right now!"

"Tear up what contract?" Maynard whinnied. "I don't know what you're talking about!"

"I'll tell you what contract — the one covering that stupid, crazy piece of property on Main Street that you hooked us with!"

Joe Maynard got to his feet, mostly to avoid the finger brandished under his snipe nose. "Why in heaven's name would you want to do that?" he countered. "Your company got a marvelous buy; it's worth three times what you paid for it!"

"Look, bub, you know damn well that property ain't worth a nickel! We were gypped and you know it!"

Maynard's helpless smile only vaguely concealed an insolent, triumphant sneer. "Why, Mr. Bailly, as I said, I haven't the slightest notion what you are talking about."

"Now look here! You do know what I'm talking about! You knew nobody could build there, let alone operate a business on the site!"

"Why *can't* you build?" Maynard exclaimed. "That corner is one of the most valuable in town! I didn't rob you . . . you robbed me! Tell me, why can't you build?"

Bailly lost the power of speech. He stood rigid, his fists clenched, so tight his knuckles showed white, and glowered. His jaws worked, the veins at his temples swelling into a jumble of purple cords. He swiveled and turned his back on Maynard. "Why? It's . . . it's haunted, that's why!"

"Haunted?"

"Yes, it's haunted, and you know it! It's impossible to tear it down!"

"Bailly," sneered Maynard, "you must be insane."

Bailly's twisting lunge carried him halfway across the desk. "Who's insane?" he shouted. "I'll show you who's insane!"

Maynard stumbled backward into his chair. "Now, look, I didn't mean . . ."

"You going to try and tell me you never heard that place was haunted? You never heard about any strange stuff going on in there?"

"Like what?"

"Like the smell of burning flesh, smoke coming out of the floor and walls, weird noises, a vicious black cat. And Maynard, did you ever hear of anyone getting choked in there?"

"Choked? No, of course not!"

"Well, buddy boy, you're hearing it now. *I* got choked!"

"*You?*"

"Yes, *me!* And nobody could see who was doing it, either! And," Bailly continued, speaking through clenched teeth as he lit a cigar, "you're positive . . . it *ain't* . . . haunted, right?"

Maynard thoughtfully considered this statement. He looked up at Bailly. "To tell you the truth," he lied, "I've never had any reason to believe it was haunted, and, for my money, that goes for *any* house!" Bailly frowned and Maynard, smiling sardonically, pulled on his nose. "What do the rest of the people over at Summit say about it? Do they think the place is crawling with spooks?"

Bailly scowled and chewed on his cigar. "I don't know how they'll take it. I haven't told them yet."

"You haven't told them yet?" Maynard grinned. "In other words, its only *your* idea that the deal should be killed." He rocked far back in his chair. "Oh, boy!" he laughed. "How I'd love to be there when you give your reasons for turning back the property! But maybe . . . maybe I'm wrong. Maybe Summit Oil *believes* in ghosts and haunted houses!"

Bailly didn't say a word. Red-faced, he marched to where Maynard's hat hung, snatched it from its place, and returned to Maynard's side. Joe eyed him suspiciously. "Buddy boy," Bailly snapped, "I want you to pay a little visit to your little old homestead

. . . *now!*" And with that he plunked the hat squarely down on Maynard's head.

Pop Allan squinted at the Boar's Head Tavern and loaded his pipe. "Can you fellows see him now?" he asked.

"No," said J.D. "I can't see him. Can you, Hank?"

"Uh-uh, he just faded out of sight like he did at school, but he must be over there someplace. He didn't go into the house; you can tell when he goes into the house by the way the ramp sags."

The absorbed way Pop and the boys had been viewing the Boar's Head was potent bait; it gathered spectators. These in turn attracted more, and now the entire fence was lined with curious onlookers, each wondering what the others found so fascinating.

Several times Jake had slouched from the building, each time casting a look in the direction Bailly had gone. Then he consulted his watch, shook his head, and reentered the taproom. The hammering and pounding continued, but in a halfhearted manner; the men were not eager to get on with their work, and Jake did not prod them.

Convinced there was nothing much to see, some of the crowd turned away from the fence, but the sight of a car containing Bailly and the terrible-tempered Joe Maynard entering the grounds changed their minds. They waited.

"Hey!" Hank exclaimed, and pointed at the automobile. "Mr. Maynard's in that car!"

"Who be in what?" rumbled a deep voice a few feet from where Hank stood. Both boys sucked in breath and snapped their faces in the direction of the familiar voice, but Teach was nowhere to be seen. "I asked ye kind and proper, lad, who be in what?"

J.D. nudged Allan with his elbow, and whispered from the side of his mouth, "Did you hear him?"

Allan removed the pipe from his mouth and frowned. "Hear who? I didn't hear anybody."

"Blackbeard! We can hear him, but we can't see him!"

Much to the amusement of the bystanders, Hank was wriggling his shoulders like an African savage doing a war dance. It wasn't funny; he could feel Blackbeard's hand on his shoulder and he couldn't shake it off.

"Look'ee, Hank," the voice growled, "quit jumping 'round like a chicken 'thout a head! Lively, lad, which o' the swabs be Maynard?" Hank stopped wriggling and the voice continued, "Are ye going to jump ship after ye gives your word to Blackbeard?" Hank remained silent, and the next time J.D. heard the voice it was a foot from his own face.

J.D. lurched against Allan, and it was only his teacher's steady hand that saved him from doing an imitation of Hank and losing his voice. When he could see Blackbeard, J.D. thought, it wasn't so bad. At least he didn't look like a ghost. But this voice-without-a-body business was awful!

"What did he say, J.D.?" Allan asked quietly.

"He wants to know which man is Maynard. He thinks Maynard is the one who is going to tear down his house. I can't tell him who Maynard is! He could really hurt him, and I'd be the one responsible if he did! Pop, what can I tell him?"

"You mean his only object is to stop them from tearing down the Boar's Head?"

"That be it, matey!" Teach rumbled.

J.D. swallowed hard. "He said, 'That be it, matey.'"

Allan knocked the ashes from his pipe by tapping it against the fence. He cleared his throat, raised his chin high, and sent his words in the direction of the Boar's Head. "Captain Teach," he said, as he opened the gate, "could you and I have a word in private?"

People stared, and as he passed through the gate, they shrank back. Twenty feet up the path, he came to a stop, and expectantly looked about. From the tavern came the crash of falling plaster and Allan wheeled, a big smile on his face. It was as if a friend had surprised him with a hearty slap on the back. Allan pointed the stem of his pipe at the porch, where Bailly and Maynard noisily argued.

"Jeepers!" said Hank, "What do you suppose he's talking about?"

His conference ended, Allan ambled back to the gate, an area that now, except for the boys, was completely deserted. "What did you tell him, Pop?" J.D. asked.

Allan folded his arms across his chest and grinned at the house, the stem of his pipe cocked between his teeth at a jaunty angle. "Nothing much, J.D. I just cleared up a few things."

"Oh," said J.D., and both boys turned startled eyes from Allan to the porch, where Jake had joined Bailly and Maynard.

"So you haven't had any more trouble?" Bailly was saying.

"Nope."

"Mr. Maynard, here, seems to think it's all imagination, Jake."

The foreman eyed Maynard scornfully. "Imagination!" he snorted. "Well, your imagination could sure get a workout if you hung around this joint for a while!" He turned toward the entrance. "Come in here and I'll show you something." He stood to one side as Maynard entered, then looked at his boss. "You coming, Mr. Bailly?" he asked. The vice president ignored him; he was carefully edging his way down the ramp. Jake, hiding his grin, shrugged and stepped into the taproom.

Halfway down the ramp, Bailly came to an abrupt, white-faced halt. Hesitantly, his hand groped before him. Then his body stiffened and he jerked the hand back as if he had touched something red-hot. From his throat came strangled sounds. Cautiously, like a man sleepwalking, he squeezed by an unseen form and staggered down the ramp and up the path toward the gate. Allan went to meet him. "Take it easy, Mr. Bailly," he chuckled as he guided the twice-stricken man to a grassy spot under a tree. "It was nothing but a ghost."

In the taproom Jake pointed at the fireplace with his thumb. "Mr. Maynard," he said, "here's an example of the trouble we've been having around here. It's absolutely impossible to . . ." His lecture was cut short by a screech behind him, and the frantic scuffle of feet. He turned in time to see an invisible force hoist Maynard by the scruff of his neck and the seat of his pants, carry him across the room to an open window, and send him sailing through.

"Jehosaphat!" the foreman yelped, and rushed to the window. Maynard had just rolled to a stop in the heavy grass. "Mr. Maynard!" Jake yelled, "are you . . ." At that instant, something heavy and solid collided with his rear end, and he too made an unexpected exit. He windmilled through the air, landing in a sprawl near Joe Maynard, who was now sitting up and rubbing his head.

Teach had tossed Maynard and Jake out a window on the far side of the house, so this bit of ghostly horseplay had gone unseen by the crowd, but much speculation was aroused when Maynard, supported by Jake, limped around a corner of the tavern into view. Dressed as he was, in a rumpled alpaca suit, his long, narrow face wearing a vacant, confused stare, he looked like a wounded undertaker.

J. M. Bailly rested his portly bulk against a tree and watched Jake and Maynard approach. Never, thought J.D. as he observed Bailly, had he seen a more malicious grin on anybody's face. But the look was wasted; Maynard completely ignored Bailly. He slapped the dust from his jacket, and sourly viewed the crowd. Jake's attitude was just the reverse. His cheeks were crinkled into deep lines, and his eyes sparkled as he squatted beside his boss. Never again would Bailly question his judgment. Never again would Jake Kowalek play the part of an underdog to J. M. Bailly! Nosiree, bub!

Allan had explained the presence of Blackbeard's ghost to an understanding Bailly, and the reason for all the trouble in the Boar's Head. Now, puffing his pipe, he wandered over to where the boys were basking in new-found glory. They were half encircled by spectators who kept a respectful distance, and who bug-eyed them with the same kind of awe they would have lavished upon two beings from another planet. To say the least, J.D. and Hank were getting to feel pretty secure and confident.

Pop had scarcely opened his mouth to speak

when from the tavern came a torrent of screams and yells, the pounding of feet, and the crash of tools. Pop's pipe almost fell from his mouth as he whirled about.

"Holy cow, Pop! Can you hear him?" cried J.D. "You can hear him, can't you, Hank?"

"Sure!"

Pop grabbed J.D.'s shoulder and pointed at the tavern. "You mean you can hear him above all that other racket?"

"Golly, yes! He's screaming bloody murder in some foreign language! Pop, he's liable to kill someone! Hank, did you see that guy fly through the window?"

The confusion mounted, and wide-eyed workers, propelled by some unholy force, were ejected from door and window, followed by their tools of destruction — sledge hammers, crowbars, even lunch boxes. From the front door lunged an air hammer, trailing its long hose. Five feet above the ground it writhed and stabbed at the crowd, jumping about like a demented python.

The crowd was too astonished to panic, utter a word, or even move. They could only gasp and stare. Hank reached over and yanked his friend's sleeve. "Look, J.D.," he whispered, "on the porch!"

"Yeah, I see him!"

Blackbeard stood on widespread feet, glowering at the crowd like a mean and hated wrestler who had just climbed into the ring.

He rubbed his nose with the back of his hand, then, catching sight of the boys, his sneer became a grin and he lumbered down the ramp. "Holy smoke!" cried a voice from the crowd. "Look at those planks jumping up and down like they was nuts!" And the boys knew they were still the only ones who could see Blackbeard.

A moment later Allan asked, "Can you boys see him?"

"Yes sir, Pop," said J.D. "He's standing right beside you." Then he added, "Hello, Captain Teach." Even Hank mumbled a hello.

"Oh?" said Pop. "Where did you say he was?"

"Right there," said J.D., pointing.

Bailly, overhearing the conversation, rose to his feet and picked his way to a position behind Allan. His thick lower lip hung and his eyes bulged.

"Pop," J.D. announced, "Captain Teach is talking to you."

"Oh, I beg your pardon, sir," said Allan, turning to the vacant space beside him, "but I'm afraid I can't hear you."

The boys saw Blackbeard frown and scratch his head. "J.D., lad, ye tells 'em for me. Tell the swabs Teach ain't swallowing no more scuttling. The Boar's Head stays as she be!"

Allan frowned as J.D. repeated Blackbeard's words. "But, Captain," he argued, "you've got to understand. The Boar's Head Tavern has been out of your hands for over two centuries; you don't *own* it any longer!" He pointed at Bailly. "It belongs to this man now . . . or rather, to his company."

It was fortunate neither Allan nor Bailly could hear Blackbeard or see his face, or they wouldn't have been so complacent. "What kind o' bilge are ye giving ol' Teach?" he roared. "What do ye mean, Teach don't own his Boar's Head?" He glared at J.D. and pointed his thumb at Bailly. "Who be this fat toad, lad, what looks like Eden and claims he owns me Boar's Head?"

J.D. pulled on Allan's sleeve; he was getting very worried. "Pop," he begged, "Captain Teach *insists* he owns it! And he's awful mad! And the way he's looking at Mr. Bailly, I don't think he should stand so close to him." The vice president blinked and backed away.

Allan scratched a match against his heel, and lit his pipe. "Captain Teach," he said, "I've read a good deal about you in a lot of books." He waved the match out, tossed it aside, and J.D. watched the scowl leave the pirate's face. He caught Allan's eye and made a sign with his fingers that indicated Allan was doing fine. "All of those books," he went on, "every single one, makes a point of telling what a great pirate you were — in fact, they claim you were the *greatest*. But, they also point out how *smart* you were . . . smarter even than Governor Eden."

He glanced at J.D., who was smiling and nodding his head. "So now, Captain, your house has been sold, but," he quickly added, "it *wouldn't* have been if we had known you were coming back." He paused, "Captain, I believe I have a solution." He puffed on his pipe a few times, withdrew it from his mouth, and said, "Why not *buy* your tavern back?"

"What's he a-saying?" Teach howled, and slashed Allan with a scornful stare. "Buy back me very own Boar's Head?" Angrily he paced the gravel path, clutching the hilt of his cutlass with one hand while the other, doubled into a fist, pounded the air. He stopped in front of J.D. and Hank, his eyes filled with hurt. "Has the man lost his wits, lads? Buy back me Boar's Head, when I ain't never sold it or give it away? Teach owns it, he do!"

He veered in the direction of the building and complained as if to someone on the porch. "Did ye hear," he whined, "what the swab be a-saying, Aldetha? They wants Teach should be a-buying back his own house!" He cocked his shaggy head. "Eh?" he grunted. "I didn't hear ye," and he clumped farther up the path to the foot of the steps.

Hank nudged J.D. "Who's he talking to, J.D.? I can't see anybody."

"Neither can I!"

Blackbeard scratched his back and tugged on his beard; his face had a dubious look. "Well, Aldetha," he grumbled, "effen that be what ye thinks. But effen the crew gets wind o' this, they be saying ol' Teach be gallied for sure!" Pinching his lower lip between his fingers, he came about and strode down the path to Allan.

"How much," he asked slyly, "does ye figger the swab will take for the leaky, shipwrecked hulk?"

J.D. repeated word for word, and Allan looked at Bailly. "Well," he asked, "how much do you want?"

"Hey! Wait a minute, Allan! This fellow is a ghost! Where would he get the money? Why — why, it's ridiculous, talking about selling a house to a ghost!" Then he paused and scratched his head. "Do you really think he's got the cash?"

Allan smiled. "I think he's got the cash, all right. After all, there is nothing on record that shows that any of his buried treasure was ever found . . . and take my word for it, he had plenty! How much would you take for the place?"

Bailly rubbed his chin. He looked at Joe Maynard and smirked. "What do you think, Joe? Wouldn't you say the place was worth . . . say, two hundred thousand?" He laughed and turned back to Allan. "We'll take it in gold doubloons. At the present rate, that would be about ten thousand of them. Am I right, Mr. Allan?"

"Yes," said Allan thoughtfully, "that's just about it." He glanced at Maynard, who was white with anger and frustration. He rapped the ashes from his pipe into his cupped hand. "J.D.," he asked, "does Captain Teach think the price is fair?"

J.D. shook his head. "He says he'll pay it, Pop, but he ain't very happy about it."

Allan was just winding up a story about the long and fruitless search for Blackbeard's gold when he was interrupted by cries of amazement, then gasping silence. He faced the tavern.

Standing on the porch, visible to everyone, was Captain Edward "Blackbeard" Teach. His beard was smoking, and the fuses sputtered and hissed. He carried in his hands two enormous sacks which swung heavily at his sides. They were mildewed and hoary with age, marked with strange red and green symbols. At his side stood Aldetha Stowecroft. She leaned on her staff and grinned up at Teach, and Diablo purred and stroked his glossy coat against her long black shroud.

"Aldetha," he chuckled, "your spell worked! The folks be a-seeing ol' Teach and Aldetha right good." He winked at a pretty girl. "It be working, Captain," Aldetha cautioned, "but ye better fergit the shenanigans and tend to your business. The spell ain't going to last for long!" Cackling her mirth, she clapped him on the back and Blackbeard headed toward the group standing near the gate.

"Here be your gold, Bailly," he rumbled,

and he poured the contents of the sacks at the man's feet. It made a substantial pile, and the coins clinked, glittered, and rolled about in the afternoon sunlight. Wiping his hands on the front of his jacket, he turned to Allan and stuck out his hand. His eyes twinkled. "Thank'ee, Pop," he grinned.

Allan felt his hand grasped and vigorously shaken by the biggest, roughest paw imaginable, while over his shoulder, Teach watched Maynard hungrily eyeing the gold coins that Bailly was scooping into the bag. His twinkle turned into a leer. Without removing his eyes from Maynard, he growled, "Be it mine again, Pop? *All* mine?" Allan nodded.

Blackbeard dropped Allan's hand, stepped back three paces, drew his cutlass, and his eyes became evil slits. "Bob Maynard," he bellowed, "ye belly-robbing rumskutch! Ye owes Teach a hunnard pounds for doing him in, ye does!"

Startled and alarmed, Maynard wheeled and saw the monstrous pirate barreling down the path like a steamroller of doom. His cutlass was aimed at Joe's midsection, and he left a trail of smoke from the burning fuses in his beard.

The skinny man blanched and backed slowly away, but the blade followed, coming ever closer. He bumped into the trunk of an elm, yelped, and froze, the point of the cutlass an inch from his nose.

A deadly silence descended; even the hooting, growling sounds of traffic died away. It was Pop Allan's calm and steady voice that broke the spell. "Captain Teach," he said, "before you do anything rash, let me offer a suggestion. I believe I have a solution."

Without taking his blazing eyes from the wilting Maynard, Blackbeard turned an ear toward Allan, who was leaning against a tree trunk, nonchalantly puffing on his pipe. "Ye got what?" he growled.

"A solution, Captain. How would it be if, instead of the hundred pounds, Mr. Maynard returned all of your furniture to the Boar's Head? Would you agree to do that, Mr. Maynard?"

The terrified man's eyes never left the business end of the cutlass. "Of course I would," he quavered, "only make him put that awful knife away!"

Blackbeard's scowl spread into a broad grin. The cutlass slowly came down, and it clattered as Teach slid it back into the scabbard. He rolled and rocked his bulk around, and on widespread legs, thumbs thrust into his belt, faced Allan, his face exuding boyish good humor. "Ol' Teach be'n't coming alongside and grappling onto a word so big as that un, Pop. It shore be a four-gun-frigate word, I say. But mark'ee, effen your 'sellooshun' mean this scrovie belly-robber be a-fixing to take the Act . . . waal . . . effen he do that, ol'

Teach be willing to sign him on any time he wants."

With that, Teach shoved his hairy paw at Maynard. "Ye wants to ship with honest ol' Teach?" There was a long pause, and then a wonderful thing happened! Maynard's long, dry, leathery face cracked into a grin and, impulsively, he took the offered hand.

Allan laughed. "Mr. Bailly, how about you? Is the Summit Oil Company 'taking the Act' too?" Bailly had been frowning in total confusion, and when he spoke, his expression didn't change.

"Taking the act?" he growled. "What act?"

"In the early nineteenth century," Allan chuckled, "when a pirate decided to turn over a new leaf and quit piracy, and get all the nice people to like him again, he 'took the Act.' Nowadays, I guess people call it 'public relations.' In your case, it would mean donating enough to put the Boar's Head Tavern back into the shape it was in three hundred years ago, and keeping it that way. Think the Summit Oil Company might be interested?"

Bailly gradually lost his frozen look. "Oh," he said, "so that's what it means!" For a moment, he was deep in thought. "You know," he mused, "that might not be such a bad idea. I'll bring it up at the next board meeting, but I'm positive they'll go for the idea. Allan . . . count us in!" He gazed at the tavern. "Never did think much of this site for a gas station, anyway."

Hank was puzzled. "What the heck are they talking about, J.D.?"

J.D. rubbed his nose with the back of his wrist. "I don't know," he said. "It's all Greek to me!"

Rubber squealed on pavement; the scream of a siren moaned downward into a growl and was silent. A young, smooth-cheeked policeman made his way through the crowd. He recognized Allan and his white teeth flashed. "Hi, Pop!" he called.

"Hi, Jim!"

"What gives here . . . some kind of publicity stunt?" He studied Teach, grinned, and looked at Allan. "Who's the clown dressed up like a pirate? Anybody I know?"

"Pirate?" Allan asked, looking around. "What pirate?"

"Why, that pi —"

Jim couldn't see him any more, nor could J.D. or Hank, or anybody else, for that matter. Blackbeard had vanished!

# EPILOGUE

# 13

It was almost a year to the day since
Blackbeard had made his dramatic purchase of
the Boar's Head Tavern. Hank and J.D. were
heading for the old building.

Hank picked up a stick and, as he walked,
held it against the picket fence. It clicked and
rattled. "Hey!" cried J.D. "Cut that out! You
want to mark up the fence?"

"Golly, no!" said Hank. "I forgot!" and he
threw the stick away.

A good many changes had taken place in
Godolphin during that year. J.D. was an inch
taller, while Hank had added almost two inches
to his already lanky frame.

But mostly it was the Boar's Head which
had been transformed. Now the building and
grounds were beautiful. Painted white, the old

house nestled amid the elms upon a blanket of smooth green lawn. Inside, the mahogany and teakwood gleamed. Near the gate, set into a huge rock was a bronze plaque which told the history of the tavern, stating that now it was a museum owned by the city, containing an exhibit of pirate lore — all, of course, about Blackbeard. It also told how the building had been restored and was operated under a trust fund established by the Summit Oil Company and Joseph Maynard. At the bottom was the name and title: "George Allan, Director."

Over the fireplace in the taproom hung a large portrait of Captain Edward Teach in all of his smoking, bearded glory; on the opposite wall, a steel engraving of the *Queen Anne's Revenge*. Above the secret door to the dungeon, in a frame screwed to the wall and covered with glass an inch thick, lived the "magic scroll." Allan and the boys had solemnly vowed never to tell a soul of the powers hidden within the mystic words and symbols.

The building was filled with Blackbeard's original priceless antique furniture, and the walls were lined with Pop's old charts, maps, and ancient prints. There was also his wonderful collection of muskets, pistols, and cutlasses.

Hank looked furtively at the old house. "It was just about a year ago, J.D. . . . do you realize that? I wonder what ever happened to Blackbeard?"

"Yeah," J.D. replied, "I wonder too. Funny, we never saw him again after that day, and nobody else did, either. And that old woman! Golly, did she ever give me the creeps!"

"Me, too!" Hank said fervently. "Blackbeard wasn't too bad, even if he was a ghost. But I can do without both of them."

"Yeah," said J.D., "so can I!"

At the gate they paused. Pop Allan was sitting in one of a group of wicker chairs on the lawn. It was shady, he had a newspaper on his lap, and the old man dozed. They watched him brush at a pesky fly that buzzed around his head.

"Hi, Pop!" J.D. called.

Allan looked up and grinned. "Hi there, fellas . . . come on in!"

J.D. nudged the gate open. Suddenly and wildly, he grabbed for the pickets and hung on. Obviously Hank didn't notice it, but J.D. did! He had seen, just for an instant, the strange action of the chair opposite Pop. Right before his eyes, the legs had been forced downward into the soft turf as if some tremendous weight had been applied to them.

Pop looked at J.D., then at the chair.

Just then, a high-pitched feminine shriek split the air. It came from the drowsy interior of the tavern, and was followed by the sliding crash of dishes breaking, and then a raucous chorus of hoarse, hearty laughter!

J.D. stared at Hank. "Holy cow!" he gulped. "Did you hear that noise?"

Hank's face was a blank. "Uh-uh," he said, "what noise?"